DEDICATION

I am dedicating this book to the lonely child who has no home, no father or mother, and no brothers or sisters to call their own. This is for the child who feels all alone, has no one to turn to, and has no shoulder to cry on. A child should have someone to share love, joy, or the pitfalls of sorrow with; someone to wipe away their tears; someone to encourage, support, or do anything they want; and someone to tell them to not be afraid of who they are. Someone to teach them right from wrong, to pick them up when they have fallen, and to show the beauty in life and the world that they live in.

No child should feel all alone. I have seen this way too many times. I hear the hurt that I hear when a child tells me that no one cares and feels unwanted. This doesn't only apply to the very young; it applies to all of us, for we all have a child living within us. Don't be afraid to reach out, for we have all suffered pain.

Captain McDoogle
BB

XXXX1

TABLE OF CONTENTS

CHAPTER 1

LOOKING THROUGH THE WINDOW PAIN

William "Bill" Schyular, a widower of eight long years, had maintained vigilance in the blanket-draped armchair by the front-room window. Ever since his beloved Sara had passed from his world, Bill's life had been one of seclusion and sadness. Through the windowpane, Bill once again could see the love of his life and the times spent together, but only through his memories. Bill's thoughts often took him to happy times of fulfillment and security. Then reality hit and wreaked havoc on his heart, and his only desire was for life to end and the pain to cease.

His house was not maintained, for his ambitions were only to be reunited with Sara. The only time he left this domain was to head into town for food and other necessities, never straying for more than an hour and always returning to the comfort zone of the chair. The front room, full of furniture that was more comfortable than his chair, brought back painful memories of Sara's loss. This room, which had not been altered since her passing, was the place Bill and Sara would pass the evenings away. Never lacking for conversation and affection, the love affair abounded between the two. Even when Sara's hair turned gray, Bill never noticed. All he could see was a woman of beauty and grace, never seeing beyond her.

As Bill was in deep thoughts, he heard a low and soft whine. He followed the sound to the outside of the back porch. It was a cold, snowy night, and there on the back steps was a dog—mostly black with ginger markings on his face and legs. He was covered in mud and ice, shivering uncontrollably. The look in his soft brown eyes told a story of neglect and misery. Bill opened the screen door to the enclosed porch and motioned for him to come on in. Slowly and weakly, he stood up and made his way through the door. He stood by Bill's side, shaking and looking up at him. For the first time in many years, Bill's compassion took hold of him and made him realize that someone once again needed him.

Bill went into the house to the hall closet and pulled out an old, thick blanket. He returned to the enclosed porch and laid out the blanket. He motioned for the dog to lie on it. It didn't take much encouragement for him to come to the blanket, and he was quick to spin around a few times and settle down upon it. Bill once again returned to his house and headed for the kitchen. He grabbed a large plastic bowl from the upper cabinet and filled it with water. He brought the water back out and laid it by the blanket. Once again returning to the kitchen, he pulled out a bowl of leftover roast and potatoes and threw them in the microwave.

After a few minutes, Bill fetched the bowl out of the microwave and headed back to the cold and starving dog. Bill could tell he had taken some drinks of water because of the water drops around the water bowl. After Bill placed the food bowl beside the water bowl, within a flash, the dog was facedown, eating the best meal of his life. While he ate, Bill thought to himself that he must be at least three years of age. By the time he finished licking it clean, he was warmer, and his shivering had stopped. With his tail wagging, he went over to Bill and sat in front of him. As he sat, he raised one of his front paws up to shake Bill's hand as a gesture of thanks. This small animal melted Bill's heart.

Bill bent down, stroked his head, and softly said, "Welcome to my world." With that said, Bill stood up and walked over to the door leading into the house, stopped, and turned around. He saw him still sitting there, watching every move Bill made.

"Good night," Bill said as he turned back around and turned out the light. The grateful animal found his spot again on the blanket and fell fast asleep.

Bill headed back to his chair, thinking to himself about what name he should give his newfound friend. He went over and over the various names in his head. Then he remembered that while he was in the Navy, a friend's parent from South Bend, Michigan, used to send him Kipper Snacks, and so the dog's name would be Kipper. With that puzzle solved, his thoughts traveled back to his beloved Sara. Through the endless memories of her, his cheeks were flooded with tears. He never tried to hold them back, considering every memory of joy. Every day was a struggle to survive without his partner in life; suicide was never ever a thought. Even though Bill's faith in Christianity was weak, Sara's was strong and never-bending. Bill knew enough to know that suicide was a sin, and he wasn't going to take any chances that he wouldn't be able to be with her after he left this world.

Bill came into this world in a family that lived on a farm not far from Volland, Kansas. With his mother Marge, his father Roger, and five siblings, times were hard, and all had to pull their own weight to share the work. There were six children all together, but little Cheri died days after being born. She was the sixth child to be born, and Bill's mother took it awfully hard and spent many hours by Cheri's gravesite, which was located on the corner piece of ground near the orchard. Bill's dad was a stern but fair man who gave little evidence of his emotion from the event. He maintained his focus on the daily chores of the farm to occupy his mind. Bill was the fourth oldest, behind two older brothers, a sister, and one younger brother. With two older brothers, Bill had to be ready to defend himself against the endless barrage of attacks when he least expected them. For the most part, this was usually taken in stride until someone got hurt or their father caught them not doing their chores. When their father caught them in this situation, he always had more chores to add to the list they already had.

He would say, "You've got no time to play. There's plenty of work that needs to be done."

Once Bill's father found them sitting behind the barn doing nothing, Bill and his brothers were quickly put to work clearing the weeds and brush from the fence that lined the pastures. With only an axe and hand sickle to work with, it was the task from hell.

When Charles, Bill's oldest brother, reached the age of eighteen, he left the farm one summer day and never returned. He never spoke a word about his desires for far-off places or wanting to leave; he just left without a goodbye. Some people felt he had left for California or he was killed somewhere along the way. No one knew for sure, and this took another toll on Bill's mother.

Leroy, Bill's next oldest brother, met and dated a young lady from the next town over, which kept Bill busy trying to keep up with the workload that was left for him and Thomas, his youngest brother. Leroy decided on his own that life with his girl was better than life on the farm. His father didn't agree with this decision but knew that he was twenty years old and could make up his own mind in such matters. His mother was indifferent to it. Leroy moved to Alta Vista and married his girlfriend. Her father got him a job at the local grain elevator.

Thomas was three years younger than Bill and kept out of sight, making it hard for their father to find him for chores. Thomas left no doubt about his lack of interest in farming. Bill's sister, Laura, attended the household chores and worked the garden.

When Charles had left, their mother wasn't much help anymore. She couldn't control her deep depression over losing Cheri and not knowing where Charles was. Her remaining time was short; by early next October, her body had withered away to nothing, and the desires of life had left her. She died in her sleep and was buried alongside little Cheri.

Bill's father was now feeling the years of his age and was slowing down to a point of almost no worth at all. Bill's father was now staying inside the house, and he very seldom left it. He was kept in the dark about the problems between Bill and Thomas. Both brothers realized that their dispute was something that their father did not need to have on his mind. Bill was doing almost all the work around the farm alone because Thomas was becoming more vocal about his lack of interest in the farm. This was causing a great deal of conflict between the two brothers. Then the day came when Bill and Thomas came to blows, with Thomas getting the worst of it. Bill was tall and had a strong figure of a young man, and he had had enough of Thomas not sharing in the number of chores that needed to be done. When the dust finally settled, Thomas made it clear that it wasn't going to be long before he would find another place to live.

Laura was keeping the household in order and ensuring their father was taken care of. Bill was so grateful for all that she did. Bill, on many nights while lying in bed, wondered how long he could continue taking care of the farm. He confided in Laura about his feelings, and she, too, wondered the same thing. Laura was in her final year of high school and had a boyfriend named John Tucker. They were talking about marriage but were unsure if he would leave for the Marines first. Bill was now in his junior year of high school but had no further plans beyond that.

It was almost a week after Bill and Thomas's fight that Thomas came home from school and held a letter in his hand. It was from Charles, Bill's oldest brother. His return address was in Torrance, California. It told about his life in California and how he had met and married a young lady by the name of Vickie.

Laura got ahold of the letter and read it over and over. It had been such a long time since they'd heard from him and the tales of his adventures in California. When Laura told her father and Bill of the letter, Bill was grateful to finally know what happened to Charles, but their father was indifferent. Their father never mentioned Charles's name after he left. Some thought that they might have had a fight, and that's when Charles left. Laura knew she had to answer Charles's letter and let him know about their mother and the health of their father.

An idea struck Thomas, which he thought might be his escape from Kansas and the farm. He knew what he had to do—answer the letter and ask to join them in California. He knew he had to try.

Weeks rolled by, and the school year ended. Laura graduated, and John was heading to the Marine Corps Boot Camp at Paris Island, North Carolina. He was scheduled to be there for nine weeks and then another six weeks at infantry training. He and Laura decided to marry upon completion of infantry training, where they would have several weeks together prior to his first assigned duty station. His departure was a sad affair. Bill, along with John and Laura, took the truck to Manhattan, Kansas, to bid him farewell. Laura was beside herself but knew this was something he wanted and would make their lives together a better place.

Once Bill and Laura left the train station, it occurred to Bill that if Thomas left for California, he would be alone to take care of the farm and his father. He knew Laura would want a home of her own and that their father would not be part of it.

He turned to Laura and said, "What plans are you making for yourself while John is away?"

Laura's facial expression didn't change, and she replied, "I figured this needed to be talked about sooner or later. Now is just as good a time as ever. I need to find a paying job and start a savings for John and me— for our future. I know that you're concerned about who will take care of Dad. Thomas got the letter from Charles that told him to come on out to California. I imagine that he will be leaving as soon as possible. And that leaves the farm and Dad for you to take care of. I know it doesn't seem fair to leave you with all the burdens, but what can we do about it? We cannot afford to place Dad in a nursing home. With all the chores of the farm and going to school, how will you be able to manage?"

Bill looked at Laura and knew in his heart that she didn't want to place all the burden on him, but she had a life of her own. "I don't know, but I have to do the best I can. The farm has always been our livelihood. Dad is hardly able to function at all. It'll all work out, even if we have to lease out some of the land." With that, Bill went silent.

As Bill drove his dad's truck, thoughts of what to do circled in his head. Laura had a long face that showed her worry for her father, brother, and the life she was beginning. Through the long drive home, not another word was spoken.

Bill pulled the 1955 Chevy pickup into the driveway and stopped in front of the peeling white-painted one-car garage. The garage had been the resting place for so many discarded household furnishings that it hadn't had a car or truck parked in it for years.

Laura got out and headed toward the house. Bill climbed out, walked over to the corral fence near the barn, and leaned on it. Laura turned and watched Bill standing by the fence, and slowly a tear ran down her cheek. She knew that no words could change the situation, so she turned and headed inside the house. Unbeknownst to Laura, Bill himself had tears filling his eyes, realizing that the shoes he had to fill were twice the size of his.

Within two weeks, Thomas had packed up and caught the evening Rock Island train down at Volland Station. He did not speak many words to Laura or Bill. He did spend some time with his father, but his dad couldn't understand anything he said. Laura was caught several times weeping deeply for her father. She contacted Leroy, and he kept the vigilance of not having the time to come and help out. She knew time was short for their dad in this world. Bill knew it too.

The daffodils were sprouting up along the fence surrounding the house. Springtime had arrived. Trees were budding, and the birds were singing their merry songs. Bill knew that Laura's John would soon be home to take Laura away. He knew that time was short for the spring planting. He set about preparing the machinery for the task.

As he was changing the oil in the old vintage tractor one morning, Laura came screaming out the side door. "Bill, Bill, come quick! I can't get Dad to wake up!"

Bill jumped to his feet and ran past Laura and into the house. He found his dad in bed, pale and not breathing, and he knew that the Lord had given him wings. Bill fell to his knees next to his father's bed and wept. Laura came in and kneeled next to her brother, crying without concern.

The following weeks were hard and heavy on both sides. Their father's funeral was held at the church and attended well. He was buried alongside Mary and little Cheri. Close friends of the family provided an after-funeral dinner at Laura and Bill's house for family and friends. Upon the conclusion of dinner, Laura and Bill met with family members. The main topic of discussion was how Bill was going to juggle school and maintain the farm. All sides were quick to point out that he would also need a job to pay the never-ending bills. Their father had tucked away a tidy sum of money, but they knew it wouldn't last too long. Bill was adamant about keeping the farm and going to school. Laura was of the opinion that they should sell the farm and Bill should move in with an aunt and uncle in a nearby town. This was not acceptable to Bill. The day was drawing to a close, and Bill went and sat on a lawn chair close to his mother's flower garden.

The following week, while Bill was at school, Laura received a phone call. It was John, and he was on his way to her. He would be arriving in Volland within a day. He was now a lean and mean U.S. Marine and had orders in hand to be stationed in Hawaii. He had two weeks of furlough, which was just enough time to get reacquainted with Laura, pack her up, and move to Hawaii. They would get married by the justice of the peace, with no time for a honeymoon. Laura's heart was full of pure joy until she thought of Bill left alone, fending for himself. How would she tell him that the time had come for her to leave? The thoughts sent terror through her veins, knowing that Bill would feel totally abandoned. She still wished that Bill would sell the farm, but she knew that would never happen.

Bill came through the kitchen door and saw the look on Laura's face. It didn't take long to realize that Laura had some bad news.

Bill softly asked, "What is it?"

Laura's face was streaming with tears. "John will be here tomorrow, and he's got orders for Hawaii." She shook her head. "Bill, sell the farm. You can't do it all by yourself!"

Bill's face turned stone cold, and he said, "I have to try!"

Laura burst out in tears, went back into her bedroom, and closed the door. Bill caught himself in a rare mood and realized that he had never talked to Laura in such a sharp voice.

Bill knew he had to change his attitude and went outside. He decided to walk down to Old Man Johnson, who lived half a mile down the road. Dad always went to him when he had to get something off his chest. Bill was sure that he could help him with what to do in his situation. Bill walked up the uneven sidewalk that led to the front door. He didn't even get a chance to knock when Mrs. Johnson opened the door and welcomed Bill in.

"What brings you down, Mr. Schyular?" she quickly asked.

"I was hoping that Mr. Johnson was available for a chat," Bill responded.

"He's out in his workshop, and I think he would be happy to see you."

"Thank you, Mrs. Johnson." With that said, Bill headed out the kitchen door and toward the small wood-clad building, which was in desperate need of paint. Bill walked up to the small side door and gently knocked. Within seconds, Mr. Johnson was opening the door and motioning for Bill to come in.

"So sorry for the loss of your father. He was a good man," Mr. Johnson said, staring into Bill's eyes.

"Yes, he was, and an even better father," Bill said, without choking up. "He taught us hard work, right from wrong, and keeping to your word. Let me get to the meat of this conversation. Charles, Leroy, and Thomas are all gone; Laura got married, and her husband, John, now is stationed in Hawaii. Laura will be leaving within two weeks. I have one more year of school and the farm to take care of, and I'm the only one left to do it all. They think I should sell the farm and move in with my aunt and uncle in Eskridge. What do you think?"

"First and foremost, what do you want out of life? I'm not talking about small things you want to do for fun; I mean, what do you want to do for the rest of your life? Do you want to go to college, join the military, or live somewhere else? What about a wife and family? All these things are more than passing thoughts. These are steadfast decisions that will stay with you the rest of your life!"

"Of course, I want a wife and family, but the question is, can I survive going to school and keeping the farm?" Bill asked, with doubt in his voice.

"You need to evaluate all the options that you have. You have an awesome farm, but it needs to be upgraded. If you sold it right now, you wouldn't get enough for it in the condition it's in. As for school, there is no decision to be made on that. You will always be behind in life without an education. You have to have some source of income to pay the bills and the necessities of life. Do I think you can go to school, work a job, and run the farm? I'm not sure. It'll be a hard road to hoe, but if anyone can do it, you can!"

"I don't want to sell the farm, and I don't want to quit school," Bill said with a heavy sigh.

"It doesn't matter what you do. The missus and I will support you in anything you do. I don't know what I can do to help with school-work, but I assure you, anything on the farm, I can help," Mr. Johnson said with a wink of an eye.

"Fair enough, and many thanks for your time and wisdom." With that said, and a hearty handshake between the two of them, Bill headed out the door and headed for home.

It was nearly dark, and the sun was almost out of sight, when Bill stopped about halfway home, crossed the ditch, and stood near the barbwire fence as he gazed across the pasture. He went to his thoughts, thinking of how hard his father had worked to keep the land and provide for his family. Bill himself had finally realized that he was alone in filling his father's shoes in keeping it all together. When he finally came back to reality, it was totally dark, and the only bright spot in the sky now was the moon. He crossed back over the ditch and went home. Laura was waiting for him on the porch swing and had the look of a worried sister for her beloved brother. She knew he had the weight of the world on his shoulders. *What would be his final decision?*

Laura stood up and walked to the edge of the porch. "How were the Johnsons?" she quickly asked.

"They were both fine," he replied. "I talked to Mr. Johnson for a short while. He was very supportive of anything I wanted to do."

"What have you decided to do? You know that you could sell the farm and come and stay with John and me in Hawaii," Laura said in a low-toned voice.

"Laura, I love you with all my heart! But you need to make the life that you and John are about to have without me. Please understand that Dad worked so hard to make certain that our life's needs were met. Sure, we didn't have many of our wants, but we never went without a need. We had clothes on our backs, food on the table, a roof over our heads, and loving parents who never gave us reasons to be bitter or sorry for our lives. Yes, Charlie, Leroy, and Thomas left to seek out a different lifestyle but not from being abused or neglected. I have another year left in school, and then I can get a job to help pay the bills. I have enough to sustain myself till then. If, after a while, I can't make the farm support me, then I'll change directions and go another way. For now, I'm keeping the farm and going to finish school."

Laura bowed her head and slowly nodded in acceptance of his decision. She reached out her arms, and Bill walked up the steps and held her close to him.

The next day, John arrived on time at the station. The joyous reunion between Laura and John was almost too much for Bill to bear. The two lovesick birds had stars in their eyes but with no notion of Bill. Never had Bill seen so many kisses before. Bill was so glad to get home, so he could make his escape from them. Within two weeks, Laura and John were on their way to Hawaii and a new way of life. The first night that they were gone was the loneliest night he ever had. He had never spent a night by himself He realized that the sounds of the house were ones he had never heard before.

The next morning, he arose from a restless sleep just in time to get ready for school. Once in school, the jarring effect of a lack of rest made him realize that the morning chores were neglected. Adding to the loneliness of being left alone, he was having second thoughts about keeping the farm. He barely made it through the day and left school with a head full of worries.

The next couple of days had blown by, and before he knew it, it was Saturday morning. He was about half asleep when there was a sharp, rapid knocking at the front door. Getting up and putting on some clothes, he answered the door. It was the neighbor, Mrs. Johnson.

"Come on in, Mrs. Johnson." Bill quickly opened the screen door. "What brings you to my humble home?"

"Yesterday, I was down at the senior center and got talking with Mrs. Davis," she replied. "She said her house caught fire last month and is trying to figure out a more permanent place to live. She has been shuffling around between friends and family. She could help with the house chores; she's a darn good cook, and she is willing to pay rent. That could help a lot with your situation. She does sew on the side for extra money."

"Yes, I know Mrs. Davis," he said with a serious look. "She helped Mom when Cheri died. I'll have to give it some thought. It sounds like a good idea, but I'm not sure I'll want an older woman coming into my house to stay."

"Here is her telephone number," she said. "She is expecting your call. Better get back to my man before he realizes that I'm gone," she said with a wink. In the blink of an eye, she was gone.

Bill closed the door and headed back to his bedroom, thinking to himself, *She is a very kind person. Mom really liked her, and she is definitely a great cook. Being an African American wouldn't matter. I guess giving a call to find out things wouldn't hurt.* Bill looked at the clock and thought that it was too early to call. He finally decided to get fully dressed and start the chores. By eleven o'clock, he had headed inside to fix a quick bite to eat and give Mrs. Davis a call. After eating a sandwich and a handful of potato chips, he grabbed the phone and dialed the number Mrs. Johnson gave him.

Within a couple of rings, the voice on the other end answered, "Hello, Nadine Davis speaking."

"Hello, Mrs. Davis. This is Bill Schyular. How are you today?" Bill said in a shy and low-toned voice.

"Why, Bill, it's been a long time since I talked to you!" she replied.

"Yes, it has," he said as he searched his mind, trying to figure out what to say next. "Mrs. Johnson came by today and said you were looking for a more permanent place to stay. I was wondering, what are your thoughts about you living here with me?"

"Well, she did fill me in on your situation. But first, let me give my condolences on losing your father. I didn't know him very well, but I do know he was a hard-working man and loved your mother. God bless her soul. I feel we could benefit each other in several ways. I can clean, cook, and do the laundry. I'll even pay one hundred dollars plus half of any grocery bills. Your life will be your own as my life is my own. It will always be your house, and if at any time you feel that I need to be gone, just say so, and I'll be gone. But one thing that I need is a room to set up my sewing machine and stuff."

Bill thought to himself that this seemed to be a done deal. "I appreciate your thoughts on my father and mother. I miss them both a lot. How about you coming over and we can look over the situation? You can have the master bedroom. It has its own bathroom. We can make another bedroom your sewing room."

She responded, "I don't need the master bedroom. I just need a small bedroom; I don't take up that much space. How about I come over after five this evening? We can iron out the plan."

"Sounds good to me," Bill said. "Thanks, and have a good rest of the day. Goodbye!" With this said, he hung up the phone. When he placed the phone on the receiver, he just stood there and gave it more thought. *She could relieve him of so much of the household chores, and he probably would be eating better. An extra hundred dollars would ease the depletion of the family's money. Should be a win-win situation.* With all that had transpired, he went about getting ready to head out to the shed and prepare to start the planting season.

He was busy setting up the equipment and tractor for spring planting. With so much to do and so little time to do it, he thought to himself that he should have done all of this last night. He now realized why his father was always on the go and trying to get him and his brothers to help with the chores. It was just about five o'clock when the green 1953 Chevy car came rolling up the driveway. It sounded and looked good for a car of that age. She pulled up next to the fence gate and got out. She looked as he remembered her, but with a little more age. He took the rag from his hip pocket and wiped the dirt from his hands. He smiled as he walked over to her.

"Hi, Mrs. Davis!" Bill stuck out his hand.

Mrs. Davis just shook her head. "Don't just give me your hand; I want a hug!" She quickly embraced him. "And don't call me Mrs. Davis. It's Nadine! Hell, I've known you since you were modeling diapers. You've become a handsome young man. But all of you boys were extremely good-looking."

"Okay, enough of that! Let's go into the house, and I'll fix some coffee," Bill said as he gestured with his hand to the house.

"Thank you, but no thanks! I don't do coffee, but if you've got some iced tea, I'll take that instead," she said as she took in the sight of the house. She thought to herself that she had never seen the place so neglected.

"I just happened to have fixed a jug of it made this morning," he said with a half-chuckle.

After they both walked in, they settled down at the kitchen table. Bill set about getting two glasses out and filling them with ice. He pulled the jug of tea out of the refrigerator and filled the glasses. He set one in front of Nadine and the other in front of his place at the table. He reached up in the corner cabinet and pulled out the sugar bowl. Within a second, he had a spoon to go along with the sugar bowl.

Their conversation lasted an hour, and then they walked through the house for another hour. It was finally settled that she would have the master bedroom with the bath. Thomas's small bedroom would be her sewing room. He promised to have it cleared out by the next day. By the time she had left, it was getting late, and he was worn out.

Bright and early the next morning, Bill set about clearing out the two bedrooms and bath. No sooner had he completed his tasks than the old Chevy car was coming up the driveway. He quickly went out to greet her. Her car was loaded to the hilt. He assisted her with all her belongings, setting them in her bedroom. She quickly went about putting her stuff away. It wasn't long until she set about cleaning up the kitchen. She quickly shooed him out the door. Realizing that he wasn't needed inside, he went back to start the tractor and commence the spring planting.

Bill's thoughts returned to reality when the teapot sounded. He had totally forgotten about it, and prior to standing up, he gave Kipper a couple of quick pats on his head. He rose from his chair and slowly strolled into the kitchen to quiet the high-pitched whistle of the tea kettle. With a tea bag already placed in the coffee cup, he filled the cup with steaming hot water, ensuring not to spill any. As Bill reached for the bottle of honey and sugar bowl, he caught a glimpse of a moment in time when Sara used to fix his tea in the morning. In an instant, Bill felt a sharp pain inside his chest. It was without a doubt to him that it was just more of his heart breaking. He thought to himself, *It won't be long now.* When the pain subsided, he finished fixing his tea. He grabbed the cup and headed back to his chair and his faithful companion. He placed the cup on the small wooden table next to his chair and sat down. Once in place, Kipper jumped up and placed his front legs on Bill's lap. Bill gave him a smile and a hug, and then he set Kipper's legs back on the floor. Being content with that, Kipper spun around and curled back up on the rug next to Bill.

CHAPTER 2

A LIFE TO SHARE

Bill glanced up at the wall and noticed that the calendar that Sara had maintained for so many years was still showing the month when she left his world. He searched his mind, trying to figure out what day it was. Without a doubt, he knew it was winter. December was still the month that hurt the worst. With his lack of attention to days, and since he did not receive a newspaper, he wasn't quite sure how to tell what day it was. He knew he had to head into town for some gas for the truck and a few items from Mike's Market. Surely, he could find a newspaper to look at and find the answer to the question of what day it was. He realized that it was still early, but he needed to find out if any of his monthly bills were due.

As Bill sat in his usual chair and stared out of the panes of glass, he was seeking a place where he felt no pain from the present day. As he stared out toward the age-old elm, his vision blurred as his mind refocused on a place and time in his past. He found himself walking the halls of his old high school, smelling the presence of the familiar papers, textbooks, and copying ink. He was passing fellow students that he hadn't seen or even thought of in some fifty odd years. It would have to be around 1965 or 1966. He recognized so many of the faces but felt that no one knew he was there. Then it happened—he spotted the small-framed girl who would later steal his heart, never to return it not that he wanted her to.

He seemed to lose his breath at the sight of her. She was standing near the locker that she had so many years ago in the hallway of their school. The school was a three-story yellow brick building with grades from first to eighth. He had many fond memories inside these walls, but the greatest one was what he was watching now. As he watched her every move, Bill thought to himself, *Is this really happening, or am I just dreaming?* He remembered this day—the day he would meet his forever love. How is it, after all these years, that these memories came back to haunt him or renew the feelings of his lost love? After a couple of large swallows, he slowly made his way toward her, never taking his eyes off her, not even to blink.

She looked his way but made no motion to indicate that he was there. Then, in a moment, it seemed as if their eyes had met, and she gave a slight smile. She tipped her head downward, and he could see her cheeks turning a darker shade of pink. She was wearing a light, flowery summer dress that ran down to her knees. Her hair was a lighter shade of brown, with a long wave across the top of her head. Not a single hair strand was out of place. As she slowly raised her head up, her light blue eyes pierced his heart, never to be the same again. *Oh, if only this was real!*

It was several weeks after this day that Bill finally worked up enough courage to ask Sara to go to the drugstore in the middle of town after school for a milkshake. From that time forward, they were never far apart. Bill would walk her home every day from school and start attending church just so he could be with her. Sara's parents didn't mind at first but were getting concerned that they were being way too serious at such a young age of seventeen. Even though Bill was fully aware of Sara's parents' concerns, this did not deter Bill from ever being with her. The time spent with her took away the pain of his own life at home. With the loss of his father and mother, his younger sister, and the abandonment of his oldest brother and youngest brothers, he had many sorrows to feel. Her gentle soul provided him with the much-needed guidance to ensure his success with his school and farm chores. She was never cross with him, even when he failed to do the right thing. Sara, being a devoted Christian, never made Bill feel less of a person. She knew this was in the good Lord's hands; Bill would finally surrender to his goodness. Within time, Bill slowly understood Sara's love for the Lord, even though he never accepted or denied him.

Lacking cash, Bill took up a job with Old Man Zimmerman, working on his farm. The old man had his nose to the grindstone and expected Bill's nose to be right there with his. At first, Bill was having a hard time keeping up with his assigned tasks, and the old man showed his displeasure with Bill, but the old man realized the determination that Bill had for his responsibility. Within time, Bill learned to complete the needed tasks at hand without being told.

Mrs. Zimmerman was a sweet and kind lady, and without a doubt, she ruled that household. When she came to the fields with dinner, everything stopped, and dinner was enjoyed. When she left, it was back to toting the bale. The old man was a fair and honest man. When it came time for pay, he never lacked in giving it out. When he handed out the pay, in the first couple of months, he would make a comment about the lack of progress in getting the chores done, but after that, he only gave comments about things that needed to be done.

The income that he was making ensured that the farm's bills were paid, but the rest he kept for doing things with Sara. Once Bill was able to save a little every time, he started considering getting a car, for he knew that without one, he wouldn't be able to get a better-paying job, and they would have to walk to every place. Dad's truck was becoming more and more of a problem with all the breakdowns. He wouldn't dare take Sara out in an unreliable vehicle.

Then came the day when the neighbor, Mrs. Johnson, mentioned to him that Widow Mary had an extra car since her husband Joe had passed away. With excitement drumming through his brain, he headed into town to her house to ask about the car. Reaching her house, Bill quickly walked up to the front door and knocked. Time went into slow motion before the door opened and the frail figure of Widow Mary stood before him.

"Good afternoon, Mrs. Nobles," Bill quickly blurted out. "Mrs. Johnson said you have an extra car you might want to sell."

Mary smiled at Bill and shook her head. "Yes, Mrs. Johnson said you might be paying me a visit. Let's go to the garage and take a look at it." She stepped through the door and led him down the driveway to the one-car, unattached garage. She motioned for him to open the garage door. Once opened, there in front of him was a dusty and dirt-covered 1954 Dodge sedan, complete with four flat tires and boxes filled with junk inside. Bill's heart swelled with joy but was quick to fade back to reality, thinking about what she would want for it.

"What do you want for it?" he asked impatiently.

"Well, you know, it hasn't run since Joe passed away. I wouldn't have a clue what it would take to make it run, but I could use some help around the house. If you would help maintain the yard and other things, you can have it."

"Mrs. Nobles, I would like to pay for this!"

"No! I don't want a penny for it. Your family has always been good to me, and I want to pay back the friendship. I think that my husband would want you to have it. Please take it with my blessings and enjoy it as my husband did."

"I don't know what to say, Mrs. Nobles." He looked at the car and then back at her. "It's more than I could ever ask for. Thank you from the bottom of my heart. You make up the list of things that you need done; I'll be here after school to work on them."

Mary gave him a large smile and had a twinkle in her eye, for she knew that was the way it should be. She said her goodbyes to Bill, turned, and headed back to the house. She could almost swear that Bill was floating on air as he made several passes around the car.

Now in a state of unbelief, he came back to his senses and started to think about how he was going to get this car home. Instead of contacting Sara first, he thought it best to get ahold of his best friend Nick to help him. He thought that he would clean it up before showing it to Sara. Nick's house was just a block away, and he would run over and get him. Within ten minutes, he was at Nick's house, knocking on the door. Nick's sister answered the door, and with a turn of her head, she yelled at the top of her lungs for Nick. Nick's face showed surprise at seeing Bill, and he quickly walked outside to see what was up. After Bill gave an exciting exposition of his new acquisition, they both headed down the street in the direction of Mrs. Nobles's house. Upon reaching the garage that held the golden egg of Bill's desires, Nick and Bill commenced removing the boxes inside the car and stacking them neatly in the corner of the garage. Bill jumped in the front seat, took it out of park, and motioned for Nick to start pushing. It did not take long for Nick to realize it wasn't going anywhere with four flat tires.

With a shake of his head, he motioned Bill out of the car and pointed down at the tires.

"Well, that was kinda silly of me, thinking we could push this with four flat tires!" Bill said, and his face turned red.

Nick spoke up and said, "How about we check the battery? Maybe it will turn over. We can take the tires down to the Philips 66 station and put air in the tires. If they won't air up, they usually have older tires there that we can get pretty cheap."

"Sounds like a plan," Bill said with a smile. "Let's get to it." He jumped into the car and turned the key. The engine slowly turned over a couple of times and stopped.

They rummaged through the garage and found the tools that they needed to remove the battery. Bill thought to himself that he could take it home and charge it. With the battery out, Bill realized that it was time to head over to Mr. Zimmerman's place and get the chores done. He put the battery in the back of the truck and took Nick home. Soon he was heading off to Old Man Z's.

It was close to eight o'clock when he pulled up into the driveway of his home. Mrs. Davis was sitting on the front porch swing, singing as she usually did. He walked up the walkway to the front porch and said, "Good evening, Nadine. What's special in your life today?"

"Did you get the car from Widow Mary?" she said with a smile.

"Yes, I did!" he said excitedly. "I got a few things to take care of first—charge the battery and fix four flat tires, to name a few. But she's a beaut! Just got done at Mr. Z's." He took a seat on the porch chair next to the swing. The sun was just an orange spot on the horizon. It was a beautiful evening, and birds were starting to wind down their daytime chorus of song. He took a look toward the barn and said, "Better get the animals fed."

"Dinner is on the stove," she quickly said. "You also got a letter from Laura. It's on the table. I'll go warm up your dinner while you feed the animals. Did you see Sara today?"

"Just at school," he responded.

After feeding the animals, he went in and sat down at the table. Mrs. Davis served up a heaping plate of meat loaf, mashed potatoes, and green beans—one of his favorite meals. With the plate empty and his stomach full, he pulled the letter over and read it.

Laura and John were doing well; John got promoted, and Bill would soon be an uncle. When he read that, his eyes filled with tears. He had never ever thought about being an uncle before. He quickly relayed to Mrs. Davis the news of Laura's pregnancy. She smiled in return, knowing that he needed such good news.

His junior year was winding down. He was working for Mr. Z, working on the Dodge, and, of course, seeing Sara. But his farm was lacking the attention that it needed. He knew he had to keep his schedule on the straight and narrow. He wasn't sure what his true priorities were, but one thing for sure was Sara. Mrs. Davis was a true blessing and the person he could go to for advice. Inside, the house was spotless, and the weight he gained was proof of her good cooking. A farmer neighbor farther down the road took over the planting and harvesting of the grain crops. It was one less thing for Bill to do, and this brought in extra money.

The school year came to an end. Bill worked for Mr. Z as much as he could, but the work at home needed to be done. Mrs. Davis made sure that Bill was well taken care of. He usually got to see Sara about three days a week, including Sundays. Mrs. Davis went to church with him and Sara. Sometimes Sara's parents would come over to Bill's house after Sunday dinner. Sara's parents, Steve and Peggy, were quickly realizing that Bill was extremely hard-working and a good person for their daughter. Sara was totally under Bill's spell and always wanted to be with him but knew the limitations of their relationship. Bill got the upper hand on the farm, yard, and outside of the house. Mrs. Davis lent a hand with the flower gardens and roses. Laura's letter came in about every two to three weeks, telling him how big her baby bump was getting.

The letter finally arrived. Bill was the uncle of a seven-and-a-half-pound boy. Josiah Keith Tucker came into this world on August 7th at nine twenty-nine in the morning. She included a small photo of Josiah, and the look on his face showed he didn't want a picture taken of him. Josiah's middle name, Keith, was also Bill's middle name. Bill got so excited that he went about the place, showing the photo to Mrs. Davis several times. He grabbed the phone to call Sara to make sure she knew the good news. Later that evening, he cruised over to her house to show her family the photo.

His senior year of school started, and now he could be with Sara every day during the week. Bill, now a strong, sturdy young man, was being highly recruited by the high school football team. He knew that would be too much to handle. Sara was helping him with schoolwork, which made it easier for him. With the Dodge in tip-top shape, he was able to pick up Sara and bring her home. At least once a week, on the way home, they would stop at the local drugstore for a root beer float. Along with the root beer floats, he would always pick up a bar of Heath Toffee for Mrs. Davis. It was her favorite. Things were settling into place, and peace and calm were the order of the day.

Just before Thanksgiving, Bill was sensing that his relationship with Sara was beyond just dating. He knew without a doubt that he would make her his wife. On a gentle November evening, sitting on the front porch swing at Sara's house, he began talking about marriage. Sara was surprised by this topic, but she knew, too, that it would happen. They talked about getting her father's approval. How would Bill make a living to support a family? How many children should they have? When would they marry? There were so many questions to be answered. Sara wondered if she should go to college after high school. Bill rejected the idea of college for himself. He had the farm to worry about and knew he could provide a good living for Sara. With his sweet thoughts of being married to Sara, Bill was floating on cloud nine.

The holidays passed by in the blink of an eye. Graduation from high school was upon them. Sara was at the top of her class, and Bill was rated in the middle. Then one day, the letter came. It informed Bill that he was being called for military service. He wondered how this could happen. He was supposed to show up at the Military Induction Center in Kansas City in less than a month. His plans and his dreams were all dashed by a single letter. How was he going to tell Sara? Mrs. Davis had gotten to know Bill quite well and knew in an instant that he was seriously troubled.

"What's the matter?" she asked as she sat next to him at the kitchen table.

"I…I've…been called to serve in the military," he said, totally shaken.

"Oh my! Does Sara know?" she quickly responded.

He looked up at her with tears in his eyes. "No! I don't know how I will tell her, either. All our plans—what will become of them?"

She hugged Bill and said, "Listen. Sara will work it out with you. If I know Sara like I think I do, this will not diminish her love for you. The two of you will figure something out. Make the positive work for you, not the negative." With all that said, Bill got up, took a deep breath, and left for Sara's house.

With the letter in hand, it was half past three when he walked up to Sara's front door. The pit in his stomach was starting to hurt even more. The door opened, and Sara immediately realized something was astray.

"Come in," she quickly replied. "What is wrong?"

As he walked through the door, all Bill could do was embrace her with trembling arms. She realized that something was seriously wrong. They embraced for a long time, and then he pulled away from her. She could see the tears in his eyes as he held up the letter.

"I've been called for military service," he said as he choked out the words.

She gasped as she suddenly realized that their plans were in trouble.

"Oh no!" she finally said. "What now? What will become of us?" She fell back into his arms, burying her head in his shoulder and crying uncontrollably. He lowered his head onto hers, his tears streaming down his face.

Sara's mother was in the kitchen, heard all the commotion, and went to them. Surprised to find them both crying, she quickly placed her hand on his shoulder and softly asked, "What happened?" as she looked down upon her crying daughter.

Bill raised his head and handed the piece of paper to her. She quickly read it, and she could feel her heart melting, knowing what this meant for the two lovebirds.

Then she added, "What will you do?"

"With yours and Steve's permission, I would like to marry Sara," he said as he held Sara closer to him. "I've got three weeks before I have to report. That should be enough time to arrange a marriage."

Sara raised her head and looked at her mother for acceptance.

Peggy nodded her head but quickly said, "Let's talk with your dad first, before we make too many plans."

Steve wasn't going to be home for a couple more hours, so she brought them into the kitchen and made a large glass of iced tea for them. The three of them sat down at the table and tried to ease the tension. Steve got home at the expected time and found the three of them at the table. Noticing Sara's red, swollen eyes, he knew something was wrong. He grabbed the fourth chair and sat down. Looking at Peggy, Bill, and Sara's faces, he wondered what it was that he was about to be thrown into. He then saw the paper on the table, picked it up, and read it.

"Wow," was all he could say.

Peggy spoke up, "Steve, Bill and Sara have something to ask you."

"Let me guess, they want to get married? Right?" he said with a slight grin.

"Mr. Richard, I promise that I will take good care of Sara!" Bill quickly said.

"I know you will, son!" Steve said as he looked at Sara. "Do you want this too?"

"As much as I love you and Mom!" came the return reply.

There was silence for several minutes. Each looked at the other, and Steve finally spoke again, "When and where, I guess, are what's next."

Peggy spoke up, "It'll have to be soon. What do you think, Bill? You got any suggestions?"

Bill just shook his head. He knew that it would be better to just leave the wedding planning up to the women. Then he thought about Mrs. Davis. "I would like Mrs. Davis to be included in this. She has been a total blessing to me, and I would hate to think that she would be left out."

Sara wiped the tears from her eyes and said, "But, of course, she will be. We all have a lot of thinking to do to get through this. Right now, I just want to thank God for allowing this all to happen." She bent her head down to pray as they all went to prayer.

They all got up from the table, and Bill and Sara headed for the front porch swing. Sara's parents stood by the kitchen sink, looking out the window. Each of them held on to each other, as they all knew life was going to change. Bill and Sara, swinging on the swing, just held each other in a never-ending embrace, not speaking a single word— just allowing their emotions to say it all. It was almost midnight when Bill kissed Sara and said his goodbyes. When he got home, Nadine was still up and waiting on the front porch chair. He was startled when he saw her there.

"Well, what happened?" she quickly asked.

When he reached her, he held out his arms to embrace her. Taken back by this emotion, he pulled him to her, and they embraced. She sensed that everything was okay.

He pulled himself back and said, "We are going to get married with her parents' blessings. We're not sure when or where yet, but it's going to be soon. I want you to be part of this. You have blessed me with so much, I couldn't bear to have it any other way."

Nadine's eyes were flowing with tears after hearing this. She pulled him back to her and gave him a hug that would rival any mother's hug.

The next couple of weeks flew by. They decided on a small wedding at Bill's farm, followed up by a barbecue-style picnic to feed the guests. Sara would stay at Bill's farm while he was away, and Mrs. Davis would stay on too. She and Sara would turn the house into a dream home. The time was running short after the wedding. Bill and Sara decided to go to Kansas City for three days for their honeymoon. Bill then left for the Army two days later. He signed up for two years and would be completing boot camp at Fort Leonard Wood in southern Missouri.

Within nine weeks, he completed his basic training and then completed infantry training a few weeks later. Sara got to attend his boot camp graduation and spent two days with him afterward. She headed back home when he started infantry training. Upon completion, he was assigned to an infantry company at Fort Leonard Wood. Then word came down that his company was being sent overseas to Vietnam. Given two weeks' leave, Bill had to give his best to Sara, for life in Vietnam was uncertain. When Bill arrived home, Sara was there to meet him at the bus stop. Tears were flowing from all four eyes. The long embrace meant that whatever happened, their love would endure. Sara's folks were waiting at Bill's house, along with Mrs. Davis. She had whipped up a feast fit for a king: fried chicken, mashed potatoes, and gravy with green beans. Peggy had made a coconut cream pie for dessert. All three women, at times, would break up, with tears flowing freely. Bill and Steve would maintain a stern look so as not to show the sadness in their hearts.

With the given time, Bill and Sara shared every waking moment together. At night, they spent it in splendid wonder and never wanted it to end. Throughout the day, Bill marveled at the updates that Sara and Mrs. Davis made. The house was decorated nicely, and the yard, with the flowers, was beautiful.

Then one morning, when they woke, they quickly realized that they had only one more day together. Sara was doing all she could to keep from totally losing it. There weren't many minutes that would go by if she wasn't embracing him. She didn't want to let him go. It wasn't fair. The next morning, Sara, her parents, and Mrs. Davis all rode in the car as they took him to the bus depot. The long goodbyes seemed to never end. Bill's shirt was dripping wet from all the tears that had fallen on his shoulder.

He had arrived at base that evening and reported in. He set about packing his gear and placing the unnecessary items in long-term storage on the base. He hit his rack at 11:30 p.m. and didn't doze off till about three, and reveille was called at 6:00 a.m. He didn't get much sleep because all he could think about was Sara. He got up and headed over for morning chow. When he arrived back at the barracks, his company was loading up the trucks to move out. The day was cool with a heavy overcast of clouds. The two-hour truck ride brought them to the nearest Air Force base. Within thirty minutes, they were loaded on the C-140 and taxiing down the runway. The plane lifted up, and they were on their way. After several stops along the way, they finally landed in Vietnam.

Within seconds of walking off the plane, he was in a full-blown sweat. The searing heat and humidity were almost unbearable. The military had placed his company in an air-conditioned barrack room to help recover from the flight. Two days later, they were on their way up close to the DMZ. Several of the men were reassigned to other companies. Bill was partnered with three other soldiers who were positioned as forward observers. They were placed atop one of the many hills in the area to watch for Vietcong movement. Their duty was to be on the hilltop for four days and back at basecamp for three days, just long enough to sleep, shower, and eat. With the weather conditions there, he never seemed to be wearing dry clothes because of his sweat or the rain.

There were times when he was assigned to a search-and-destroy platoon. They usually lasted several days in the jungle. He came under fire almost every time he was on patrol. One night, when they were settled in for the night, they were ambushed. Outnumbered three to one, they held their position. Joe, the closest man next to him, was instantly killed. They quickly called for reinforcements. For three and a half hours, bullets whizzed by Bill's head. All of a sudden, the bullets just stopped. Of the twelve men in his platoon, three were killed. It wasn't until Bill got back to basecamp that it dawned on him about the loss of a good friend's life, how it could have been him, and how that would affect Sara.

Sara had recently gotten a job at the local bank in Alma. She really enjoyed the amount of people she got to meet. The bank manager was quick to realize how good she was with all the customers. One morning, Sara awoke and felt funny. She couldn't figure out the feeling but couldn't seem to wake fully. She walked into the kitchen, where Mrs. Davis was fixing some breakfast.

"What can I fix for you, honey?" Mrs. Davis asked.

Sara gave a face of horror. "Nothing for me, please. I'm not feeling good."

"What's the matter? Do you have a fever?" Mrs. Davies asked.

"No, just feel really strange," Sara said as she sat down at the table. "Food just doesn't sound good to me right now."

"Oh! I bet I know what's wrong," Mrs. Davis said with a giggle. "You are pregnant! Bill has been gone for over two months."

"Oh, my God! Do you really think so?" Sara said as her face went blank. "I've got to call Mom. She will freak!"

Mrs. Davis gave out a loud laugh, went over to Sara, and gave her a huge hug. Tears were now streaming down Sara's face. She rose from her seat and headed to the phone. Within a second, Mrs. Davis could hear Sara talking about the chance that she was pregnant. She heard her tell her mom that she needed to make a doctor's visit to confirm it.

It wasn't long before Sara headed out the door to the Dodge. She left a trail of dust as the car blazed down the long driveway. Mrs. Davis set about doing her normal chores that she did every day. She thought about how Bill would react to the news. Several hours had passed when Sara came back home. The smile on her face said it all—she was pregnant. Sara went immediately to Mrs. Davis and gave her a kiss and hug. Sara went into the dining room and pulled out a pen and paper from the buffet cabinet. She sat down at the table and wrote out a four-page letter to Bill. She stuffed it in an envelope and sealed it with a kiss.

Bill was on a search-and-destroy mission in the dense jungles of Vietnam when they were suddenly ambushed by a large group of Vietcong. Rocket fire came raining down on them as bullets came from all around. Bill, now a veteran of five months in the country, took cover and returned fire. His captain took a hit and fell where he stood. He was mortally wounded, so he couldn't move back to a safer position. Bill knew he wouldn't survive in his position; he jumped up and ran to him. Quickly picking up his captain and throwing him over his shoulder, he ran back to cover. It was a complete wonder, with all the bullets and rockets going off, that they missed their mark on Bill. Once in a safer location, Bill continued his return fire. Then it happened: a live hand grenade landed in the middle of his platoon. Not giving it a second thought, Bill jumped over to it and tossed it back. As he stood up to toss it, he was hit by a bullet in his lower left side. Out of commission and with his bleeding uncontrollable, he lay there as the medic tended to his wounds. The rocket attack and bullets ceased. A total of four soldiers, including Bill, were seriously injured. The platoon called in for a helicopter evacuation. For Bill, it seemed like forever before they arrived. Once placed inside the helicopter, Bill passed out.

Sara and Mrs. Davis were sitting on the front porch swing when the black sedan came down the long driveway. Mrs. Davis had a bad feeling about this. When the two uniformed soldiers got out, Sara's heart stopped. Both Sara and Mrs. Davis stood up when the soldiers walked up to the porch.

"Mrs. Schyular?" one of the two officers asked.

"Y-Y-Yes!" Sara replied.

"Mrs. Schyular, your husband, William, has been injured in Vietnam. He is alive and is in the process of being transferred to the Veteran's Hospital in Topeka. He will be back in the States within the next couple of days. That's about all I know."

"What happened to him?" Sara asked in a shaky voice. "When will I be able to see him?"

"I'm not sure when you will be able to see your husband, but I'm sure within the week. I don't have any information about his injuries or what happened. Here is my card, and you can reach me with any more questions that you may have. The country is grateful for the service your husband has done and your support of him. We have to leave you now. Once again, don't hesitate to contact us with any questions. Goodbye." With that said, the two soldiers turned and walked back to their car.

Sara and Mrs. Davis could only watch as the car drove away. Sara broke down and cried as Mrs. Davis held her in her arms.

Bill arrived at Forbes Air Force Base in Topeka, Kansas. Within the hour after his arrival, he was being checked in at the Veteran's Hospital in Topeka. Sara arrived just an hour later. When Bill saw Sara, it was all the nurses could do to retain him in his bed. The encounter was one for the ages. Kisses abounded, followed up with never-ending embraces. Talk was at a minimum, mostly words like *love* and *missed*, and then Bill noticed the baby. Bill was beside himself about their new baby. Within a few days, his mail finally caught up with him, along with the letter that Sara sent with the news of the baby.

With Sara by his bedside, his wounds healed, and he was able to get out of bed. During his time away, Sara had brought into the world a baby boy named Justin. His time in the Army was nine months. He was laid up at the hospital for five months, and the Army decided to reassign him to Fort Riley for ease of cost to the government. With only ten months left on his enlistment, he was assigned to the motor pool to shuffle personnel around base. One day, as he pulled up to a bus stop, three officers and one enlisted man were standing there waiting for him.

"Private First Class Schyular, we are here to take you to the base commanding officer's office. Private Jones will take over with the bus. Please come with us," the senior officer said.

"What have I done?" Bill asked anxiously.

"Oh no, you haven't done anything wrong, but we are not to tell you anything more," the officer replied.

They rushed him over to a waiting car and zoomed over to the base commander's office. When they got to his office, he was waiting outside with his yeoman.

"Private First Class Schyular, it is my profound honor to tell you this. You are to report with your whole family to the White House by next Thursday. You are to be presented with the Congressional Medal of Honor for heroic action during service in Vietnam. Congratulations." With that said, the commanding officer held out his hand.

"I really don't understand," Bill said as he shook his hand. As he was searching for words, he blurted out, "I just did my job."

Upon the acceptance of the Medal of Honor, Bill told Sara that so many more soldiers deserved it and about the ones who didn't come home alive. His advancement to the grade of specialist came with the medal, which meant more income for their family. After surviving the activities that came along with the medal, Sara, Bill, and Justin went home. Bill placed the medal, along with the certificate, in a small cardboard box and placed it in the hall closet on the top shelf.

Not much was ever said about the medal at home. On base, Bill was given a do-nothing job within the commanding officer building and was always called on for any VIP visit. Bill despised being placed on a pedestal. The bank held open Sara's position, and it was good to have Bill close to home. He was able to be home on Friday evenings and didn't have to leave till Sunday night. The next ten months went by fast, and with Sara having the baby, things were good. Bill was honorably discharged and returned to the farm.

CHAPTER 3

REASONS UNKNOWN

Bill got back into the swing of things on the farm. Sara and Mrs. Davis were taking care of Justin, the house, and the outside gardens. Bill started doing odd jobs outside the home, and with Sara working at the bank, they refused to take Mrs. Davis's money. A few years quickly passed, and things were good. It wasn't long before Sara became pregnant once again. In nine months, she gave birth to a healthy baby girl named Julie. Life with Sara was always an adventure, and sometimes things were extremely hard to handle. While raising the two children, when it came time to decide where to eat, going on a vacation, or just deciding how to arrange the furniture, someone was not happy. Life with a loving wife, healthy children, and, of course, Mrs. Davis,—it was as it should be.

One day, while carrying Julie from outside, Sara came across Mrs. Davis sitting in the front room and holding her chest. Quickly placing Julie in her playpen, she rushed over to her.

"I can't breathe," Mrs. Davis said as she gasped for air.

"Try to rest easy, and I'm calling an ambulance!" Sara said as she reached for the phone. She quickly explained the details to the other person on the line. After hanging up, Sara went back over to her. She held her hand and tried to calm her. It wasn't long before they heard the ambulance screaming up the driveway. Bill had gone to help a neighbor but could hear the siren. He jumped in the truck and raced over to his house. When he got home, they were placing Mrs. Davis in the ambulance. Sara was in tears; Julie was crying and wanting out of the playpen. Justin was in the backyard playing in the sandbox and came around to see the ambulance with all the flashing lights. Bill loaded the family up in the car and followed the ambulance to the hospital. It was almost an hour before the doctor came out to explain.

"Nadine Davis has passed away from an apparent heart attack," the doctor explained. "Are you the next of kin?"

Sara buried her head in Bill's shoulder while holding Julie. Justin was holding Bill's hand.

"No, but we know her kinfolk. We will contact them." Bill knew the pain of losing people close to him, but it didn't make it any easier with the loss of Mrs. Davis. That was one of the hardest nights that the family had ever had to deal with. Julie and Justin were constantly asking for their Nanny Nadine. At one point, Bill had to leave the house and go behind the barn to cry. The thoughts of her caring for him, Sara, and the children were almost more than he could bear. The funeral was full of beautiful flowers and was attended by almost the whole town. Everyone knew Nadine Davis. Her family was grateful for all that Bill had done for her. With her family's blessing, she was buried alongside Bill's mother. There, he could take care of her grave, as she had taken care of him.

The adjustment to life without Mrs. Davis was particularly hard for Sara. As she worked at the bank, taking care of the children, the household chores, and everything else was taking a toll on her. Bill, likewise, had taken on any and all extra jobs to help with the expenses of farm life. Between the two, they were making enough to meet the bills, but at the expense of Sara's health. Bill, realizing the burden that Sara was under, decided to take a more permanent job. He got hired at Smithton Publishers as a binder. He had to work the midnight shift. He was at work from 11:00 p.m. till 7:00 a.m. It was hard not to be with Sara at night, but she could get some rest. Sara's parents took the kids during the day so Bill could sleep. Sara would pick them up when she got off from the bank. The evenings were spent together as a family. This worked out fine for the time being.

Within years, the children were getting to school age, which meant many evenings attending school functions. Sara wanted to ensure that the children were able to pursue activities of their interests. Bill's jobs were never-ending, but the needs of the family were always met, not so much as the wants. Bill and Sara's offspring, a son, Justin, and a three-year-younger daughter, Julie, had little care for their beleaguered father. Justin was raised in a home where his father worked seven days a week, never spending any quality time with him, which made Justin self-efficient in all that he wanted to do. Bill, still working at Smithton Publishing as a binder, was unable or too tired to attend the majority of Justin's childhood events. With Sara attending to the household chores or being involved with all the activities that Julie was part of, she herself didn't spend much time with Justin. Growing up within an exceedingly small community in Kansas called Alma, Justin was fending for himself and regretting his life alone. Justin considered this no life in his small-town world, and upon his completion of high school, Justin moved over seven hundred miles to Dallas, Texas. He never bothered to look back and only talked to Julie on rare occasions, one of which was his announcement of getting married. Bill was never even considered for a phone call on this subject.

Julie never really established a relationship with her father; she was always closer to her mother. With her father never home much, she spent lots of time with her mother doing household chores, watching TV, and, of course, going shopping. With the occasional family outing, Bill was never much in sight of her. Upon entering high school, Julie became ever increasingly absent from the home front; either school activities or the presence of a boyfriend kept her busy through three short years. Upon graduation, Julie decided that home life was somewhere other than her parents' house.

Within a year, Julie met Clint, and after a very short love affair, she left her father's house and married her newfound love. They moved fifty miles east to Silver Lake, Kansas, to be closer to Clint's work at MoKan Construction Company. Julie took a position at Dr. Johnson's Family Medical Clinic as a receptionist. Within a year, they brought a beautiful, bright-eyed young girl into their lives, Samantha. Life was great and full of laughter and joy. Their lives seemed to be fulfilled, but with the passing of Julie's mother, Sara, Julie failed to realize that she had forsaken Bill. Julie only called occasionally, especially if there were needs to be filled. Bill hadn't gotten to meet Samantha—Sam—until she was almost eight months old. Since that first meeting, Bill had only seen her a handful of times. As with most marriages, the excitement of the newborn baby, who was now ten years old, was wearing off. The laughter and joy were absent in the house.

Unbeknownst to Bill, life had taken turns in the wrong directions for his forgotten family. After being married for sixteen years, Julie was starting to wonder if her life was at a dead end. Clint and she had placed so much distance between them that the miles would be nearly impossible to make up. She had suspected for a few years now of Clint's unfaithfulness, and even though she knew of this situation, she cared less about it. She caught herself noticing and fantasizing more and more about the various good-looking men with whom she came into contact. The main reason they hadn't called it quits was more of a convenience than a relationship. Clint was gone more and more with his construction job, and this had not been a problem for her.

At the ripe old age of fifteen, Sam realized a few years earlier that her parents' relationship was quickly dissolving, and she distanced herself from them. With her illusion of a perfect family gone, she filled her void with an association of fellowship with other youths in the community. As with the dissolution of the family, so were Sam's attitude and reputation in her own town. Sam had no problems finding cigarettes, booze, or drugs to support her escape from her life's sadness and struggles.

The more involved she became with this lifestyle, the more she withdrew from any type of respectability. She was blaming every type of authority, skipping school, and performing every type of disobedience possible. Her parents were not aware of or even concerned about Sam's actions. Finally, the top blew off the volatile situation when she was caught in a mobile home on the edge of town along with four other youths. The home belonged to a twenty-three-year-old by the name of Josh. In the mix of these people were the commodities that provided the escape from reality. The authorities located drugs and illegal contraband valued at over a million dollars. Even though Josh wasn't present, an arrest warrant was quickly issued and set into motion. Due to the seriousness of the types and amount of drugs found, the four were now facing felony drug charges. They were taken into custody and turned over to the juvenile authorities. Due to the severity of the crime, the courts would not allow them to be released to their parents.

A court hearing was set for the next day at 9:00 a.m. With all present—with the exception of Sam's dad, Clint—the judge wasted no time in coming to the point. Not one to mince words, the judge quickly proclaimed them all adults. It was going to be hard to face prison time at the age of fifteen. Julie was shaken back to reality and realized she neglected her daughter; it dawned on her like a ton of bricks that Sam could be facing prison time and it would be her fault. The judge adjourned the court for two weeks for the family to set up a defense for the accused. After hiring a lawyer for Sam's defense, the lawyer who took the case immediately notified her that Clint needed to get involved. Julie knew that the situation was way beyond her and quickly informed Clint, who said he'd be home that afternoon.

Julie was finally allowed to see Sam at 3:00 p.m. that afternoon. Julie was fighting back the tears as she was escorted to the room where Sam was waiting. Sam's face was hanging down with her hands tucked under her legs, never once looking up. Sam was sitting on one side of a table, and Julie took the chair across from her. Julie could just look at her daughter and think about how things turned to this. She went through her mind of Sam's life from birth to now. By now, the tears were flowing freely.

The room was brightly lit, and uneasy feelings were vibrating all around the two figures who sat facing each other.

"Sam, I know I'm a horrible mother, and this has led you to this place," Julie said as tears dripped onto the table. "I know I'm to blame, and I'm lost for answers to the solution you need."

"Spare me, Mother! It's too late for confessions of sins. You never bothered with me before. Why bother now?" Sam loudly snarled back at her.

Julie was totally taken by surprise from this outburst. Never had Sam spoken to her this way; Julie was speechless. A whirlwind of thoughts and emotions poured through her mind. Knowing she had to keep her wits about her, she laid aside all thoughts with the exception of finding a solution to Sam's problem. With the attitude that Sam was having with her, it was not making things easier.

"Sam, you can hate me all you want, but I've always loved you, even when it seemed that I didn't. You're facing some serious trouble, and we need to figure out how to get through this. Your father should be here within the hour; I hope he can help figure some of this out."

"*Oh great!* That's all I need is to have someone else tell me how bad I screwed up." With that said, Sam started to cry. With tears flowing from both of them, Clint walked into the room. He took a few steps into the room and stopped. He looked down upon his little girl and realized how much she had grown. Clint wondered to himself when the last time he saw Sam was. Even though he had been home several times this past year, he couldn't remember seeing Sam or even giving her a thought. A lump in Clint's throat was growing to the size of a baseball. He was choking back the tears when he decided to speak.

"Hi, Sam. Hi, Julie. I'm sorry we have to meet under these circumstances."

Julie wiped the tears from her eyes and gave a slight nod of her head. Sam just gave a quick glance to him and returned her head back down, facing the table. Clint quickly realized that this conversation wasn't going to be easy. He moved around the back of Julie and pulled a chair away from the wall and up to the table. Clint was sitting down when their lawyer walked in, carrying a stack of papers two inches thick. He walked around to the other end of the table, pulling another chair away from the wall. He dropped the paperwork on the table and sat down.

"Samantha, my name is Dwight Miller, and I will represent you in your case. I must first explain to you the procedures that you will have to follow. Before I start, do you have any questions?" he said, without a smile or even giving Julie and Clint a look.

Sam just shook her head no and kept staring at the table.

"Well, first off, you know the judge deemed you an adult, and with the seriousness of the crime, this has been filed as a felony charge. Do you have any idea how serious this is?"

Sam just sat there with her head looking down.

"If I'm going to help you, you need to open up to me so we can make a plan that will keep you out of prison. Right now, you're looking at upwards of fifteen years in prison." When he finished saying that Julie lost control of her emotions and wept loudly. Clint was finally shaken by the reality that this was not going to be a slap on the wrist; it was hard time punishment.

She looked up at him with an expressionless look and said, "I'm screwed. What kind of defense could you possibly give to help me?"

"Let's try and look at the cause of your actions of missing school and hanging out in a drug den for starters, if we can show the court that circumstances beyond your control led you to living this type of life."

Clint sat up in his chair and loudly spoke out, "I'm not wanting to air our dirty laundry of our lives where everyone can hear it!"

Julie quickly snapped back, "Dirty laundry? You're worried about people finding out about our miserable life when our one and only daughter is facing prison time? Right now, nothing is more important than Sam! Quit thinking about yourself and think about how we, and I mean we, have betrayed our daughter. She needs us now more than ever."

"Oh, since I've worked so much to provide for the family, it's my fault that Sam has gone astray," Clint said bluntly. "You were the one with her at home! I never heard of any problems when I sent home the money. Now, all at once, we got this problem, and we are fixing the blame!"

Mr. Miller held up his hand to stop the sparring of Sam's parents. "This is not helping the situation at all. You two need to leave the room, so I can talk with Sam."

"We are paying your bill, so don't tell us to leave the room!" Clint replied, slamming his fist down on the table.

"If you don't leave the room, I'll get someone to remove you," Mr. Miller quickly responded.

"Come on, Clint. Let's leave and think about how we can help Sam," Julie said as she grabbed his arm. Clint quickly pulled his arm away from her, turned, and gave Mr. Miller a stern stare. With that said and done, they both got up and walked out. After several minutes, Mr. Miller looked down at Sam. He could see the torment in Sam's eyes and realized the cause of it all.

"Sam, I'm starting to understand. From what I just witnessed, I can see some of what you have dealt with," Mr. Miller said.

Sam looked up at him. "How could you even begin to understand my situation? What my life has been these past five years? I don't feel any love or joy. I feel not wanted." Sam began to sob uncontrollably.

Mr. Miller got up and left the room. Within seconds, he returned with a box of tissues. He pulled out a couple and handed them to her.

After trying to dry her eyes, she continued. "I have no one to hear my voice—to share my life or hold me and comfort me in moments of despair. Lend their support or share their knowledge of life." Sam then stopped talking and bowed her head.

"Yes, you are right. I haven't had your type of life, but I do know the feeling of not being heard and sometimes not being able to share my life's joys and sorrows. So let me help you. I need to know the complete ins and outs of your life. What you tell me is just between you and me. Your parents will not hear about anything you tell me."

Sam looked back up at him and said with tears in her eyes, "Can we talk tomorrow? I need to have some time to think things over."

"Yes, I'll schedule a time tomorrow. Remember that I need to have enough knowledge of your life to show that it wasn't your fault. Wait right here, and someone will be in to get you. I'm sorry for your situation and way of life." He then got up and left the room. When he reached the doors that led outside the correctional center, Clint and Julie were standing by some old oak trees by the sidewalk. As he walked up to them, Clint saw him coming and was working up for a confrontation with him. Mr. Miller saw the look on Clint's face and took a deep breath, knowing what was coming.

"Before you start, Samantha is the first and foremost important thing. We will not get anything done by worrying about airing dirty laundry. The only chance Sam has is to show Sam's lifestyle. Let's go get some coffee, and let's decide what's best for Sam," Mr. Miller said.

With fire in Clint's eyes, he quickly said, "We have to do it without putting my marriage to Julie out on the street."

Julie interrupted, "What are you thinking? Sam is looking at prison! Doesn't she mean anything to you?" Julie broke down and started crying.

"Of course Sam is important to me, but at what cost?" Clint snapped back.

"From what I've witnessed, it's no wonder that Sam feels unwanted. What caused this animosity between you two?" Mr. Miller said as he shook his head.

"You watch what you say!" Clint said as he got in Mr. Miller's face.

"It's true, Clint, and you know it. You have spent the last eight years away from home, only to showing up when it's convenient for you. You only showed up for one of Sam's birthdays," Julie said as she choked back the tears.

"Now wait a minute. It's not all my fault. You were with her the whole time; why didn't you seen the problems that Sam was having? Did you ever call me and let me know of the situation? Were you always out dancing the night away when you should have been home with Sam?" Clint said in an irritated voice.

"At least I was with her a whole lot more time than you ever considered. We are both to blame. You're so selfish; why can't you admit it? Yes, I should have seen the problems. Maybe if you had been the father of our child, this would have never happened. All I know is that I will do anything to keep her from going to prison, even letting the world know of our dirty laundry," she said with eyes dried from tears and fire flickering in them.

"Okay, I admit it. I'm a bad father. That's not going to change the past," Clint said.

Mr. Miller piped in, "How about we go down to the park and find an area where we can gather our thoughts and work out the details to help out Sam. I think we have gained ground on the problems; now we have to find the solutions." Both of them agreed and headed down to the small city park.

The sky was clear, with a slight southern breeze blowing in. The giant guardian

trees that surrounded the park were gently swaying. The lawn was perfectly manicured, and the flowers were showing off their brilliant array of colors. Clint, Julie, and Mr. Miller were at ease with this peaceful setting. They came across a picnic table nestled in among some of the large trees in the park. They all took a seat and enjoyed the moment.

The silence was broken when Julie spoke. "Why can't life be as peaceful as this? Life is sometimes so unfair. I wish Sam could be here with us to enjoy such beauty. Let's get this worked out, so in the future, she can see some of the world's beauty too." Both Clint and Mr. Miller nodded their heads in agreement.

Clint softly spoke, "What do you need from me?"

"We don't need to name names. We have to show that Sam was living in a home where there was a lack of stability. We're not going to say one of you is to blame; it's a combination of several things. Let's look at Sam's situation. This is how I see it. You both work, and Clint, you were mostly away from home. Julie, you work a nine-to-five job and are tired when you came home. If either one of you was having extramarital affairs, that's your business and is not going to be mentioned. What does have to be mentioned is the lack of involvement with Sam. Let me say that Sam is just as guilty as you two are. She could have thrown up a red flag when she was having problems communicating with either one of you. We need the court to see that Sam's problems were not only at home but at school too. Peer pressure is one of the hardest problems to overcome, especially at her age. So, most of the problem that I see is her environment. Let's pursue the court that if we can get her out of her environment, she can be turned around and become a benefit to her community, family, and most of all, herself."

Julie looked at Clint and then at Mr. Miller. "Do you mean move away to another state?

"That doesn't work for me!" Clint said as he made a disgusted face.

"That's not what I'm meaning. Take Sam away from her environment, not yours. I feel that if you take away the one thing that's permanent in her life, it will totally throw her deeper into despair. Your home is a secure place for her. Maybe not now, but it's real, and it'll always be there. If you take that away, she'll blame herself for losing it. What would she have to come back to? I say send Sam to a distant relative to live—a change of school, friends, and a new set of rules to live by. She doesn't need a military school or very strict rules to live by; she just needs a home of love and understanding, one where she can reboot her priorities of life. A place where she can release her true feelings and frustrations. This may not sound good to either one of you, but she needs to be away from you both for a short while."

Julie's face turned into total shock. "No, not now. I need to make up for all my shortcomings. I will not live without my baby girl. I've been wrong before, but I will change. I will not permit such action. I will not hear of it!"

Clint stood up and walked a few feet away from the table. Facing away from Julie and Mr. Miller, he placed his hands in his pockets and took a deep breath.

He then spoke, "We have to do what's best for Sam. I don't have any answers to solve Sam's problems. If this would keep Sam from prison, I say let's do it."

"There has to be a better way!" Julie said as she stood up and walked next to Clint.

Clint turned and looked into Julie's eyes. He could tell she was being torn apart from her thoughts of Sam. He took his left hand out of his pocket and pulled Julie to him.

"I am so sorry that I haven't been a husband to you and a father to Sam. Things look so different when you ignore your responsibilities and seek out adventures of selfishness. I put my family life on autopilot and thought it would always be right. I know now that Sam needs us to do what's right and be the parents that she always needed."

"But how could I live with the thought of mistreating Sam and not having her near me? How can I show her how much she means to me?" Julie said with tears streaming down her cheeks.

Mr. Miller spoke up, "It will be hard at first, but I feel if things work out, she will realize that the love you have for her is sending her away. Do you have anybody who could take Sam in? It'll have to be far enough away to remove her from her so-called friends. We're not sure if the judge will allow this to happen. We will all have to ensure all of our T's are crossed and our I's are dotted. Our game plan has to be straight with all concerned."

Clint softly asked, "How about your dad?"

"He's in his sixties!" Julie proclaimed.

"Okay, how about your cousin Shirley? She has six kids of her own. I could try my cousin Jimmy, but I haven't talked to him in years," Clint responded.

"It seems we agree to try and get Sam out of her environment. Start making phone calls and try to find someone willing to take on Sam. They must have strong minds and understand the situation with Sam. Sam will not be a willing participant in this at all at first."

Julie, still being held by Clint, nodded her head in agreement. She pulled herself away from Clint and walked over to Mr. Miller. Still sitting at the table, he looked up at her, knowing that this was tearing her apart. She held out her hand, and Mr. Miller took it and gave her a quick handshake. She turned and walked away without a word. Clint then took off after her, knowing that he needed to be part of this solution. Mr. Miller folded his hands together on the table and wondered if this was going to work. He knew this was going to be his toughest case. With the thought of a sixteen-year-old looking at prison, he couldn't fail this one.

When Clint and Julie reached her car, Julie turned to him and said, "I'll make as many calls as I can. I'll let you know if anyone will take Sam in. What are you going to do? Are you going to stay at the house?"

"I'd like to, if that's all right," he replied.

"I would like that," she said as she opened her car door.

"I meant it when I said that I wasn't a good husband to you," he said as he quickly grabbed the car door.

"We all have our skeletons in our closets," she said as she winked at him and got into the car. With the door closed, she started the engine and backed out of the parking spot. He stood there for several minutes as he watched her pull away. Thinking to himself what a fool he was, treating her the way he did. A tear filled his eye, knowing that the best he ever had was gone.

The next couple of days were busy for Julie, who called everyone she could think of, to no avail. Every evening she cried herself to sleep, knowing that if she failed in her quest to find someone to take in Sam, the worst thing would come to pass. Clint was staying at the house, which was very calming for her, but with no one to help her with Sam, it made her a nervous wreck. On the third day, exhausted by the last name on the list, Julie broke down and cried.

Clint, trying to be somewhat comforting to her, finally said, "Please give some thought to calling your dad. Who else do we have to try?"

With tear-soaked red eyes, she looked back up to him and said, "The way we have ignored him all these years, why would he ever be willing to do this for us? He doesn't even know Sam. I'm not sure if I even have the strength to call him. I couldn't handle the rejection if he wouldn't."

With the window curtains open and the shade half-pulled down, Bill sat motionless, staring through the windowpane, searching through his mind for a reason for life. Unaware of Kipper's head lying in his lap, Kipper sat waiting for any signs that Bill was going to move. Then the unexpected happened: the phone rang.

CHAPTER 4

WHEN TWO LIVES COLLIDE

The phone on the small single-stanchion table rang out. Bill, in a daze of days past, looked at it in amazement. Bill had had the phone ever since he lived there, and he wondered who would be calling him. He slowly stood up and made his way to it. He reached down and picked up the handset.

"Hello," he said.

"Dad, this is Julie," she said in a trembling voice.

Bill started to wonder why she was calling him. "What's going on?"

"Dad, Samantha is in really big trouble, and I need your help," Julie replied.

Bill was silent but could hear from her voice that this was serious. "What has she done?" he said with an irritated voice. He thought to himself that she hadn't called him in the past several years, and now that Sam has gotten herself into trouble, she wanted him to bail her out.

"She had been skipping school and was found in a drug house with over a million dollars' worth of drugs. The courts want to prosecute her as an adult, and if they find her guilty, she'll go to prison. Dad, I know I haven't been a caring daughter to you, but this isn't Sam's fault, and I'm the one to blame. The attorney thinks the court might accept a deal to release her to someone responsible outside the local area. Dad, you are the only one that I know that can do the job," Julie said as she started to cry.

Bill stood motionless and searched his mind for answers to questions he wasn't expecting. Bill had a pit in his stomach considering the thought of a sixteen-year-old girl, whom he had only seen on very rare occasions, coming to live with him. She wouldn't have a clue about him, and most of all, he didn't have a clue about her. Although Bill was sensing a responsibility to Sam as a grandfather, not having any exposure to her, he still knew that he must get down to the straight facts of this situation.

"I guess I should come and meet with you and Sam and see what's the best way to handle this problem," Bill said in a low tone. "Where can I meet with you?"

"Thank you, Dad. She is in Topeka at the Shawnee County Detention Center," Julie said as she choked back the tears. "When would you be able to come?"

"Tomorrow morning, I guess," Bill said as he searched his mind, trying to figure out what day and time it was. "It's too late to be able to make it tonight."

"Okay," Julie said with a voice lacking any type of life. "I'll see you tomorrow, and, Dad, thanks."

Bill stood motionless as he heard the last words Julie spoke. He couldn't remember once that Julie had ever thanked him for anything. Maybe he never listened to what she had to say to him before. Before he knew it, he realized that he was hearing the buzzing tone of an empty phone line. He slowly lowered the handset and placed it back in its saddle. Then it hit him: his granddaughter Samantha was in serious trouble, and now they wanted him to bail her out after not hearing from them for several years and then having this thrust upon him. Bill thought to himself, *Should I have told her no? What would Sara do? Why would they all of a sudden want my help?* Bill slowly made his way into the front room and sat in the chair that he hadn't sat in since Sara had left him. He gazed up at the family portrait mounted on the wall of him and his family.

He loudly spoke, "Sara, what am I to do? I've only seen Sam a couple of times, and then it was when she was really little. Why does Julie feel that only I can help? She's never needed it before." He looked closer to the portrait and stared into Sara's eyes. Her eyes almost told him that it was a chance to gain back the love that he lost so many years ago. He settled back into the chair and maintained his sight on her picture.

Bill opened his eyes to the bright sunbeams flowing through the window. As he looked around, he noticed Kipper at his side. He had fallen asleep in the chair and was truly stiff and sore from his sleeping position. He got up and walked into the kitchen to check the clock. It read 6:17 a.m., and he realized he'd better make his coffee, take a shower, and find some decent clothes to wear. He didn't know what had come over him, but he was feeling different this morning. He wasn't concerned about Sam in any way, just that maybe now he had purpose in his life.

Bill got ready, drank his coffee, patted Kipper on the head, and headed out the door. As soon as he reached his truck, he noticed storm clouds were gathering over in the west. He thought to himself, *I wonder if it's going to rain. I hope I get back before it does.* Taking one last glance around the April sky, he hopped into the old green Chevy pickup and fired it up. Within seconds, he was heading off into a world he didn't know or even want. He made it to town and stopped at the local convenience store, where he got gas, a donut, and another cup of coffee to help settle his feelings of uncertainty. With the completion of the tasks at hand, he once again was tooling down the highway, making his way to his destiny.

Within less than an hour, he was in Topeka and located the county jail. Luck was with him; Julie was just getting out of her car. Bill drove by and gave a short honk of the horn to get her attention. She gave a slight wave and stood on the sidewalk. He found a parking spot not too far from hers. His nerves were starting to work on him, and he felt a baseball-size pit in his stomach. He regained his composure, took a deep breath, and stepped out of the truck. He walked over to where Julie was standing.

"Morning," he said as he got within a few feet of her. Watching her for any sign of emotion would reveal her feelings about seeing him for the first time in many years.

"Thank you, Dad, for coming," she was quick to reply. Bill could immediately tell that Julie had spent a long and sleepless night by the way her eyes appeared. "I'm at my wit's end about what to do. This is not good, and it's all my fault. If only I—"

Bill held up his hand to stop her from further self-bashing.

"Let's not dwell on what should have happened, and let's concentrate on doing what needs to be done today. I'm sure there's enough blame to be put on all of us for our past mistakes. Right now, we have a young girl inside here who feels life isn't worth living. Let's ensure her that we love her and will do whatever it takes to make her life enjoyable once again." Bill was taken by surprise by what he'd just said. It wasn't something that was preplanned; it just flowed without thought. He thought, *Is it Sara talking or coming from my own heart?*

"Okay, what's going to be our first thing we have to do?" Bill asked, looking through the tears in Julie's eyes. Julie tried to speak but failed to do so. Bill took a few steps toward her and placed his hand on her shoulder. Julie was taken back by this gesture; for the first time, she felt a strange sense of strength from his touch.

She found her inner strength and spoke, "We got a meeting with her lawyer in about ten minutes. He's going to go over the case against her and the possible results." With this said, Julie began to get upset again. She buried her head in his chest, wrapping her arms around him. Sobbing uncontrollably, she spoke with a trembling voice, "Dad, it's all my fault! My one and only child and I lost her. I was too caught up in my own desires, not once thinking of the greatest gift ever given to me!"

Bill was quickly taken back by this rare emotion; he slowly wrapped his arms around her. He softly whispered in her ears, "We all have made mistakes in our lives; the truth of the matter is to do the right thing and work on healing from the pain from it. Come now, let's go meet with the lawyer."

Julie released her hold on him, backing away from him while rubbing the tears from her eyes. Nodding her head in agreement, she headed for the courthouse's north entrance doors. Bill paused for a moment, looking toward the heavens, looking for a sign from Sara.

Within minutes, Julie and Bill passed the check-in desk and were led into a small room with a rectangular table and four chairs. The room was brightly lit by one light fixture mounted on the ceiling. The room was as plain as they got; no pictures or any type of decoration could be found. Other than the table and chairs, there was a tall, locked cabinet in one corner of the room. Bill thought to himself, *Where is the two-way mirror that you always see in the movies?*

Julie turned and faced Bill. "Dad, I'm scared."

He nodded his head and replied, "Me too."

Within a few minutes, the door opened, and a tall, slender man walked in. He quickly set his briefcase on the opposite end of the table from Bill and Julie. He looked at Julie, then at Bill, and back at Julie. "I'm Todd Watson, and I've been assigned to take on your daughter's case."

"Where is Dwight Miller?" Julie asked in a panicked voice.

"The firm thought I could handle this better. You do have the right to choose any lawyer of your choice." He then turned his attention to Bill, speaking with a carefree attitude and an air about himself. "Are you a relative of the accused?"

Bill's eyes flared, and he quickly fired back at such an attitude. "That so-called accused is my sixteen-year-old granddaughter Samantha! My name is Bill Schyular, and you'd better show more respect to my family!"

"Well, Mr. Schyular, we are dealing with very serious problems with your granddaughter. Let's not start any problems between us! Ms. Roberts is my client, and she is who I will deal with."

Julie quickly jumped in, "This is Samantha's grandfather, and you'd better understand that you will answer to him equally! Besides, I don't think you will be the right lawyer for Sam's case. I only want Mr. Miller to represent Sam. So, if you don't mind, please excuse yourself and remove yourself."

Todd's facial expression changed to total shock at this outburst. He then quickly gathered up his belongings and left the room. Bill and Julie went back to the clerk of the court's desk and rescheduled to meet with Sam and the lawyer the next day at 1:00 p.m. They walked outside together and stopped at Julie's car. Nothing had to be said. Julie just fell into her father's arms and wept.

By 1:00 p.m. the next day, Bill and Julie were waiting once again in the room when Dwight Miller came walking in. After the introductions were complete between Bill and Mr. Miller, Mr. Miller focused his attention on his briefcase. After opening it, he pulled out a stack of papers a half inch thick. "Samantha has five federal charges and eight state charges facing her. With the exception of two of the state charges, she is facing prison time on all the rest. Since she a juvenile with no other violations other than truancy, the prosecuting attorney is willing to entertain dropping the charges to probation if we could get Samantha away from the toxic environment that she was in. This is the agreement that the prosecuting attorney had drawn up.

"She must live more than fifty miles from any other family members and must not meet with any family member or previous friends for a minimum of six months. She must be in the presence of the assigned guardian any time she is away from the assigned residence. The assigned residence will be inspected by a state official to ensure assigned residence is within standards set by the state of Kansas. A State of Kansas Department of Social and Rehabilitation Services (SRS) inspector will visit the accused every week until it is determined that the need for weekly inspections can be prolonged to longer intervals. The cost of care and provisions is the responsibility of the family of the accused. It is with the exception of the accused that Bill Schyular, the grandfather of the accused, will be the residence guardian. By this order, the court will entertain the permission to release the accused into Bill Schyular custody for a period of one year, during which the accused will be reevaluated for release from legal obligation. Any violation of this court order within a year, the accused will be brought back before the court and be tried on all charges from this court case.

"That, with a few other proposals, is the agreement; any comment?" Mr. Miller asked as he dropped the stack of papers on the desk. "If you agree to these terms, we will see the judge at 3:00 p.m. and find out if he or she agrees with the terms."

Julie looked at Bill and then nodded her head. "I won't be able to see Sam for at least six months?"

"Yes! Remember, that is, if the judge agrees with this," Mr. Miller replied.

"If the judge does agree to these terms, how long will it be until she is released to my authority?" Bill said, looking at Julie. He could see in Julie's eyes that she was starting to wonder if the judge might refuse this.

"First, you must have your house inspected, and once it has been declared a safe residence for Samantha, maybe a week or two. You know how the government loves the paperwork," Mr. Miller finally said with a half-hearted grin. "It's getting late, and I know you two will want to meet with Samantha. I've arranged a short meeting between you all, so you can talk this over with her. If you like, I'll have her brought in now."

Bill now realized that Mr. Miller made a lot of effort to get all of this done. He stood up, walked over to Mr. Miller, and held his hand out. "I am truly grateful for all you have done for my family."

Mr. Miller took a hold of Bill's hand and gave a firm handshake and a nod of the head, and he left the room.

Within a few minutes, the door opened up, and a female law enforcement officer walked in with Samantha, following closely behind. Her head was hanging down, with her hair covering her face. She was dressed in orange coveralls with white tennis shoes. Bill was taken by surprise at how much she had grown since he last saw her. The officer pulled one chair out from underneath the table and motioned for Samantha to sit.

Then the officer faced Julie and asked in a firm voice, "Is your attorney going to be present?"

Julie just shook her head slowly to indicate "No."

"Do not open the door; just knock. I'll be outside in the hall if you need anything." As she turned to leave, she gave Bill a quick glance and left the room.

"How are you doing, sweetheart?" Julie said in a low tone, as if ready to cry.

"Are you kidding me? How am I? Is that supposed to be a joke or what?" Samantha yelled.

Bill was not used to hearing children talk to their parents in that type of language and quickly spoke up, "We're here to help you! You need to calm down and be a little more respectful."

"Who in the hell are you?" Samantha growled again.

"This is your grandfather," Julie replied.

"Oh, I get it. The grandfather who never came around, didn't have anything to do with us, but is now telling me what's what since I'm in trouble. No thank you. Go crawl back under your rock and leave me alone."

The words that were spoken were carving his heart to pieces, and Bill began to realize that this might be a very serious mistake on his part. He wasn't used to youth talking to elders this way, and he wasn't about to change his way of thinking. He decided it was time to leave this situation and stood up. He had tears filling his eyes but forced them not to fall. He spoke as he started to take a step toward the door, "My services are no longer needed here, so I bid you two farewell."

Julie, now in a full-blown cry, jumped up and grabbed Bill's arm. "Dad, don't go! She doesn't know the whole story between us."

She turned to Samantha and said, "It's not his fault! I kept you away from him. I wanted just you, your father, and me to be our only family. Not that he wasn't good enough, but I didn't want any guilt from him for not measuring up to what he expected of me. He gave me and your Uncle Justin a good life and a good home, with food for the table and warm beds to sleep in. It came at a high price that only now do I appreciate. He had to work six and sometimes seven days a week, and when he wasn't working, he was doing the chores. He didn't have time for himself because he gave the remaining hours to us. He's a great father, and he's here to help us get you out of trouble. He won't if you don't let him."

With that said, Julie wrapped her arms around him and whispered, "I love you, Daddy."

Bill let loose his tears. He was speechless, and with his heart in pieces, he wasn't sure what to do next. He calmly pulled Julie away so he could look into her tear-swollen eyes and said, "If she wants me to help, I will; if she doesn't, I will have to go."

Julie turned to Samantha with a look of desperation and said, "Will you forgive me for not letting you know your grandfather? He's a good man and has never ever let anyone down that he promised to help. Please understand that life is not always fair, and the people we hurt the most are the ones that we love the most."

Samantha could tell by the look in her mother's eyes that things were not always on the up and up, but now things were out in the open. Samantha had often wondered about her grandfather on her mother's side but never bothered to push the subject with her. She looked over at Bill and said, "I guess this wasn't how you expected to meet me. I'm screwed, and the law wants to put me away. How do you expect to help me through this mess?"

Bill realized that she had opened the door for conversation with him, and he wasn't going to lose the moment. He sat back down in his chair and took a moment to gather his thoughts. Julie's tears were still flowing, but she found the strength and moved her chair closer to her father and sat down. A slight smile emerged on her face at the thought of Samantha and her grandfather talking.

"First and foremost, the courts don't want to send any minor to prison. If there's a chance, this would be a one-time thing. Second, we will have to show the reasons why you felt you didn't have to attend school and why you were caught in a house as a place to hang out and not a place to get drugs. Third, you're sorry for any problems or inconvenience that this has caused with local authorities, school officials, and the courts. Fourth, return and complete your remaining years in high school with grades that the courts find satisfactory. Fifth and finally, this will mostly be a decision where you will have to fully agree to the terms, or the deal is off. Come live with me as a means to separate yourself from anyone associated with this problem. That means living by not only the rules of the court, but the rules set by me by living under my roof."

Samantha's face was one of total shock. "I don't think so! First off, you might be a total looney who I just met. School isn't my thing, and I don't see any reason to subject myself to more rules and regulations. I just want to be clear of this mess and get on with my life." Sam just shook her head in disbelief.

Bill realized that she must be made aware of her situation if she landed in prison.

He took a short pause and commenced to explain the facts of prison. "Okay, let's compare the situation that I proposed and what your reply was. Living with me, you will have your own bedroom, take a bath in the privacy of a bathroom, choose most of your meals, watch TV, and enjoy walking around outside without someone watching your every moment. I am not a looney—I'm your grandfather.

"Now, let's take a look at your life in prison. You will probably have to share a cell with other inmates who just might be looneys, which adds to the lack of privacy. You just might have to sleep with one eye open all night. You will have to eat what is given, take showers with several others at the same time, and be able to go outside when they say you can. The people you will associate with are those they decide can be your friend. Your life is not your own; they will control your every movement.

"Freedom is very precious, and once it's gone, you can never get it totally back. If you get convicted of a felony, it's on your record for the rest of your life and will haunt you forever more. If we can convince the courts that you will change for the better, they might drop the charges under the conditions of what I propose. Now it's up to you to decide. If you decide to take a chance on me, you will have to stick with it, or they'll bring you back and charge you with everything they can."

Bill sat back in his chair and looked over at Julie. Her face had an endless flow of tears streaming down her cheeks. He nodded his head at her, and she gave a slight smile back at him.

Looking up at Bill and in a low, slow tone, Sam spoke up. "What kind of rules would you set for me?"

"Nothing more than the rules that your mother had to follow, and she survived. You will have to do your part of the chores around the house. That would be to wash the dishes, cook some of the meals, do your laundry, keep your room clean, vacuum, help with the lawn, and do anything else that I feel needs to be done. Then you will study your homework every night, respect what is mine, and never ever talk back to me. You have to get approval for anything you do outside the home and any friends you might want to associate with. Most of all, you will attend church on Sunday."

"Church. I don't go to church!" she said in a blast of fury.

Bill gave what could be called a browbeater and spoke, "God knows that I haven't been a devoted Christian since your grandmother, Sara, left this world, but he has answered many of her prayers and some of mine. Understand the Book of Laws makes life more meaningful and provides a way of life based on love. I don't think you realize that it's not only you that has to change; I too need to change. I see you as a descending angel coming down to help me with changing my life and bringing meaning back to it. Life without your grandmother has al- most been unbearable, and I feel deep down in my heart that we were made to bring each other out of the pits of despair."

Sam was quick to sense the seriousness of this conversation and broke the thought with a change of subject. "When you say to do the dishes, you mean by placing them in the dishwasher, right?"

"Don't have a dishwasher," Bill said with a grin.

"I don't know how to cook, do laundry, or any of the other things you mentioned," Sam suddenly replied back.

"I guess it's about time you learned," was Bill's response.

"I told you that school and I don't get along," Sam said as she looked into Bill's eyes as if to say, *I'll fail at this task.*

"I don't expect you to do this all by yourself. I'll be there with you every step of the way; it won't be easy on any part of this, but together we will get through this. For you, changing your way of life will be the hardest thing you will probably ever have to do. Fear is only the lack of knowledge. As with life, the more you know, the less you fear it. School is providing you with knowledge, a social life, and the structure of how life's rules must be obeyed to be successful. People hide from life because they don't understand life. Some use drugs, and others use video games to give them an escape from it. Successful people seek the knowledge to attack life head-on and live life to the fullest. This is what I've only wanted for my children and you."

When Bill turned and looked at Julie, her face was in total disbelief. For once in her life, she had come to realize that her father was a man of true wisdom. Her tears had stopped, and in her heart, she knew without a doubt that Sam was going to be all right. She also realized that, in all the years of living under his roof, she had failed to take notice of his knowledge. She now knew that she should have asked the questions of life with him.

With a short knock on the door, Mr. Miller reentered the room. "Samantha, are you willing to go along with the terms of living with your grandfather? We will be in court at three o'clock, and the judge might not approve these terms, or they could add more restrictions on them."

Sam looked at her mom and grandfather and nodded her head in agreement.

"Samantha, please understand that we are doing everything we can to keep you from going to prison. For Lord's sake, when the judge asks you a question or talks to you, give your best effort to be understanding and give courteous responses."

With another short knock on the door, the female guard reentered the room. "I have to take you back to the holding cell. There's a state

SRS agent waiting to talk to you before you have to be in court." Samantha slowly rose from her seat without showing any signs of emotion.

Julie spoke up, "It'll be all right. I love you."

Without even looking up, Sam headed out the door with the guard right behind her. Julie and Bill sat there motionless, wondering if things would really work out. Bill closed his eyes to focus on what Sara would do. He knew that she would be there for him in any situation, but he really needed her now. Bill then realized that it was getting late and thought that Julie and he probably needed to get something to eat before court.

"Let's go and get something to eat," Bill said as he stood up.

"Don't think I can eat anything; my stomach is tied up in knots. You go ahead and go; I'll meet you in court. Don't forget, it's at 3 p.m.," Julie said with her head bowed down. With that said, he turned and headed out the door.

Bill stopped at a favorite hamburger joint and then headed back to the courthouse. For some unknown reason, trying to find a parking spot was almost impossible. He drove around the area for almost five minutes before he located one a half block away. As he walked the distance, he noticed Julie was sitting on the retaining wall outside the courthouse.

"Are you waiting on me or just waiting?" Bill asked as he walked up to her.

She smiled and nodded her head. "I was hoping this was the way you were going to come. Dad, what is your gut feeling about all this? Do we really have a chance?"

Bill looked Julie in the eyes. "If I know anything, I know that we always have a chance. I am putting my faith in Sara having a talk with the Big Guy to help us out. We got about fifteen minutes before court, and I don't want to be late."

Bill held out his hand to help Julie up. Bill motioned for Julie to lead the way, and he would follow. Upon entering the courthouse and passing through the security check, they proceeded to courtroom number four. When they entered the room, no one was there.

Bill and Julie thought to themselves, *Is this the right courtroom?*

As soon as they sat down, Mr. Miller came in. "Glad to see you here already; most of the time, the main people come in late. Julie, will your husband be present?"

She just shrugged her shoulders and looked at him with a look of despair.

"You know, the judge might not make a determination today without him."

Julie's heart just sank upon hearing this. Julie quickly pulled out her phone and called him. The phone rang for a long time before he picked up.

"Clint, where are you?" Julie asked in a nervous voice.

"What do you mean, where am I?" Clint replied in an irritated way.

"Clint!" Julie said as her voice turned into rage. "Sam's court case is in less than fifteen minutes! The judge will require both of us to be present! If we both aren't present, it could prolong the process by months! Don't you care if Sam might go to prison?"

"Julie, I'm sorry; I forgot," Clint said, at a loss for words. With just a click, Clint was gone, and all that was left was the dial tone.

Julie thought to herself, *What a jerk!* If she hadn't have been that same type of jerk, Sam wouldn't be in this situation. With eyes filled with tears, she shook her head in disbelief.

"Dad, I have a bad feeling that Clint won't make it to the court proceeding," Julie spoke in a shaky voice, not knowing what else to say.

Bill stood there by Julie's side. He placed his arm around Julie and softly spoke, "We can only wonder why people do the things that they do. We can never make them do the things that need to be done. The most important thing for us to do is make sure Sam never feels that she is all alone to face this by herself. I wouldn't want her to feel that it's her against the world."

Julie slowly nodded her head in agreement while wiping the tears from her face.

"Come, let's get to our seats," Bill said in a reassuring voice.

Julie led the way, with Bill trailing close behind. Bill's mind quickly left reality, and he soon had Sara's vision in his mind. She was extending her arm as if for him to embrace her. Her soft eyes were tugging at Bill's heartstrings. Her look was a reassuring sign to Bill that he was doing the right thing. When Bill came back to the current situation, he could feel his eyes swelling with tears. Julie quickly took notice of the expression on Bill's face.

"What's the matter?" she asked.

"I just had a vision of your mother," Bill slowly replied. "I know she is with us."

"I know she is too," Julie said in a trembling voice.

Bill and Julie found seating in the second row. Sam was escorted in and placed at a table in front of the judge's bench. Sam's head was bowed down, with her hands together in her lap. She had on the typical orange coveralls with her hair pulled back in a ponytail. She never looked back at them. As soon as they sat down, the court orderly called out for all to stand for the judge's entrance. He proclaimed that the Honorable Judge Janice R. Hanstan was residing. Once the judge sat down, she started to sort out some paperwork on her desk. She called the orderly to call the first case. The moment came that Bill and Julie were waiting for.

The orderly called out the words, "Case of The State of Kansas versus Samantha Arlene Roberts." The orderly then proceeded to motion for Sam to stand.

"Ms. Roberts, have you been read your rights, and do you understand these rights?" the judge asked.

Sam just stood there motionless and didn't reply.

"Ms. Roberts, I will not allow you to refuse comment unless you plead the Fifth Amendment. Do you wish to plead the Fifth Amendment? If you do, you will not have the chance to make any comments on your behalf. Do you understand what I just explained to you?" the judge asked as she studied Sam's facial expression.

Since Sam made no motion to respond, the judge then took her stare to Sam's counselor.

"Counselor Miller, I'll allow you a few moments to ensure that Ms. Roberts fully and completely understands what's at stake here."

Julie had been holding onto Bill's hand, and with what the judge had said, her hand was squeezing hard now. Bill also sensed the moment that Sam froze.

Within a few tense minutes, Sam's attorney turned and faced the bench. "She understands, your honor, and will make her statement."

Sam then looked and spoke in a soft, quiet tone, "I understand."

The judge's face seemed to lighten up a bit, and then she spoke. "Ms. Roberts, you're sixteen years old, and I'm sure this is a little upsetting for you. You are in a situation that could easily put you in prison for seven to ten years. You were caught in an illegal drug house with over a million dollars of illegal drugs. Not only that, but your blood test also showed you had illegal drugs in your system. This is very alarming to me, considering your age. With all this, you are now considered a drug dealer, or even worse, you have the ability to get these drugs without a job. These are very serious implications, considering the cost of the type of drugs that were found in your system. You missed so much school; you will not graduate into your junior year. I do not find it totally all your fault; I wish for Clint and Julie Roberts to face the bench."

Just as they finished calling them out, Clint came walking through the doors. He walked by Julie and Bill and didn't even give them a glance. Julie released Bill's hand and got up. She walked up to where Clint was standing and stood by him. Once again, the judge fixed her stare on Clint.

"I'm glad you showed up in time for your daughter's court case. Is this the way you have supported your daughter's crisis in life, Mr. Roberts?"

Clint did not respond to her and stood there motionless.

"Before I get into the seriousness of your daughter and the drug house, I want to get your response to why nothing was done about her missing school. First, you, Ms. Roberts, what have you done to correct this situation?

Julie cleared her throat and said, "I had a few calls about this, and I talked with Samantha about it. She said she would not miss anymore."

"What about you, Mr. Roberts? What actions did you take on this matter?"

Clint was starting to show signs of nervousness. "I was unaware of her missing so much school, your honor."

"Oh, boy! You two don't have a clue about how the system works, do you? You two just showed that the most precious thing in life is a child's life that is given to you, to love, protect, and nurture through all aspects of life and ensure they are ready for their adult life. Mr. and Mrs. Roberts, I have Samantha's school record here in front of me. Mr. Roberts, there had been twelve calls to your cell phone and two answers with hang-ups. Ms. Roberts, there were eighteen calls to your cell phone, four conversations, and one hang-up. Twenty-one calls to your house phone with no answer. You two, tell me how anyone can get ahold of you in case of emergency? And believe me, Samantha is in an emergency situation, don't you think?"

Julie then just crumbled to her knees in full hysterics, tears flowing freely with this. Clint looked down upon Julie, who at one time thought that he would never do her harm. Now realizing the damage that had been done, he bent down and took hold of Julie. Tears were now welling in his eyes, and he gave Julie a gentle hug. Both knew that they were to blame for Sam, not knowing what to say or do.

The judge knew she hit a chord with so few words and said, "I will allow another ten-minute break before we continue."

Julie walked back to Bill, sat there without saying a word, and cried. Clint took a seat in the front row and stared at Sam, shaking his head in disbelief at what he was part of.

It was closer to fifteen minutes before the judge reentered the courtroom. Once everyone got settled down, the judge began to speak.

"I'm starting to understand the full situation of this case. The environment that Samantha was part of was nothing short of toxic and lacked any amount of love and care. If her parents had been responsible for Samantha, they would not have allowed her to miss school. By not missing school, she would not have been hanging around the wrong crowd. I chose to seek counsel on this case with a senior advising judge. We both agreed that Samantha, being an adult, knew what she did was against the law and must pay a price for her actions. We also agree that she was not totally to blame. I have here in front of me a proposal that might reverse the effects of the environment that brought her to this court. It was drawn up by both the state of Kansas and Samantha's attorney. I have fully studied this proposal, and for the most part, I agree that this might be what Samantha needs, but with some changes. Samantha, her parents, and Mr. Schyular, please face the bench."

CHAPTER 5

RULES TO LIVE BY

The bailiff escorted Sam to the front; Julie and Clint were next to her, and finally Bill made his way to the front. The judge looked up from the papers that she had in front of her.

She first looked at Bill and said, "Mr. William Schyular, I questioned this petition on behalf of your age, being single, and being willing to take on a sixteen-year-old whom you hardly know. I know she is your biological granddaughter, but to my knowledge, you have had little or no interaction with her at all. I'm not judging your integrity or knowledge, but what do you know about raising a teenage girl with serious problems facing her?"

"Your honor, I may be old, and I may have been lacking in my duties as a father and husband, but I do know that I will not make the same mistakes that I've made in the past. I have many friends to call upon on subjects that I don't have the necessary knowledge, such as raising a teenage woman. She will never be neglected or abused. She will be given the rules of my home and will ensure that she follows them. I will abide by the rules of the court to the fullest extent. I swear this on my wife's grave."

"This is what I needed to hear. I will accept this," the judge decreed. "These are the changes that I will make to this proposal. If all parties agree to them, then we can move on."

Sam stood there motionless, her head facing down. With Julie standing next to Sam, Bill could sense Julie's trembling and Clint's state of shock. Samantha thought to herself, *The judge said changes, what changes? Nobody said anything about changes! This cannot be good!*

"Ms. Samantha Roberts, do you understand the charges against you? You are the first to either agree or disagree with these changes. If you disagree, then the court will move on to charge you with the crimes that you have committed. Do you understand this?"

Sam looked up at the judge and said in a quiet voice while nodding her head in agreement, "I do."

"Then, under the provisions set forth in this proposal, I feel six months is not long enough time to not have any communications with either of your parents. I will set the separation at twelve months."

Julie could feel her knees turning to rubber and tears filling her eyes.

"You are not to have any communications with anyone from the area where you were living previous to this date for one year. You will not be in possession of any phone or computer of any type without the authorization of this court or the persons in guardianship over you. You will be assigned by the state of Kansas a social worker who will visit you every week to check on your environment, health, and any needs that are not met. You are to return to school to finish your remaining three years of school. The local authorities and the school that you will be attending will be notified of your situation and the requirements that you must follow. Any, and I do mean any, violation of this court order, and you will be returned to me in this court, and all charges will be reinstated. The provisions that I am describing to you must be fully understood; the charges waged against you will be suspended, not removed. Ms. Roberts, make no mistake that you are a very lucky person who has people who love you and think you can turn your life around. Do you agree to these changes?"

Sam looked at her mom and then back to the judge. "Yes, your honor."

"Mr. Clint Roberts and Ms. Julie Roberts, you are the parents of Samantha Roberts. This is almost a case of child abuse, or more so, child neglect. Due to the age at which Samantha had committed the crimes stated in the warrant, I will not pursue charges against you. You are fully responsible for any costs incurred by Samantha's lodging, clothes, and food. I am placing on you the additional cost of court and the previous cost of her interment. The cost will be totaled up and presented to you within a week or so. If you had taken the responsibility of raising a child more seriously, we wouldn't be having this talk now. Do you have any questions about what I just told you?"

Clint and Julie just looked at the judge, and both shook their heads no.

"Mr. Schyular, are you fully aware of all the responsibilities that you have agreed to?"

"Yes, your honor," Bill boldly answered.

"Do you feel you have the knowledge to properly raise a teenage granddaughter, fulfill her every need, and understand her emotional needs, both the highs and lows?"

"Your honor, if I may, from what I have been told of Samantha's life, both good and bad, I can ensure the court that she will have my full attention. While living with me, she will never have a need but, without a doubt, many wants. My life in the past seven years has had no meaning. Now I feel that I can do my loving wife's mission to help my granddaughter with the love that my wife had. I beg the court to let us proceed to help Samantha in her time of need."

The judge's facial expression changed from serious to a less serious expression of understanding. "I feel what you just said was totally from your heart, but you need to hear it from the court from all aspects of what you're taking on. First, if she is abused in any way, she will be brought back to me, and you will be charged with child abuse. If the social worker feels that you're unfit, are not providing a proper place of residence, or are refusing access to Samantha or your home, they will cancel this agreement. If you have a concern or problem, you can notify the court clerk and file it with her. You need to keep an open dialogue with the social worker. Don't hesitate to contact her first. Do you solemnly swear to uphold this agreement in the case of Samantha Roberts?"

"I do, so help me, God!" What was just said shocked Bill more than anyone else. He had never thought of himself as a godly man.

"So, let's move on," the judge said. "From this moment on, let's work in a positive way and set the next couple of weeks. Ms. Samantha, you will be transferred to a state-run care home. You will be there until Mr. Schyuler's residence has been determined to be a clean and safe environment. The social worker should be inspecting Mr. Schyuler's home and depending on the amount of work needed to get it up to standards, we will determine how soon you will be released to your grandfather. Does anyone have any questions before I pass judgment on this case?"

Julie slowly raised her hand.

"Yes, Mrs. Roberts."

"Can I have a short period of time with Samantha before she is taken away?"

"Mrs. Roberts, I will allow a fifteen-minute period with your daughter. This will be open to you, your husband, and your father. I'm sorry, but that is about all the time I can give you. I don't have the personnel to support any more time. I have more court cases to deal with. One last word, Mr. and Mrs. Roberts: whatever problems you have in your household, you need to get them solved. It has been a reflection on your daughter and on how she has been directed toward wrongdoings. She is paying the price for being in the environment she was raised in. If there are no questions or concerns, I pass judgment on Ms. Samantha Roberts to be released to Mr. William Schyular for one year. The federal and state courts are in agreement with this action, and any violation of it will revoke this agreement and all charges will be reinstated. On this date, the fourteenth of May in the year of our Lord. Case dismissed."

There was a feeling of great relief when this was said. The bailiff came and escorted Samantha out the side door. Julie reached out to Samantha, but the bailiff waved her hand as if to say that was not allowed. Julie quickly turned to Clint with a look of sadness in her eyes. Clint looked down upon her, not knowing what to say.

Bill grabbed ahold of Julie and said, "Let's go find out where we can meet with Samantha. I don't think we want to lose time with her."

Julie looked up into her father's eyes and nodded her head in agreement.

The three of them walked slowly down the side aisle and out into the hallway. They stopped in the hallway and wondered where to go now. Within a minute, the bailiff had returned to them.

"If you all will follow me, I'll take you to where Samantha will be."

The bailiff turned around and walked down the long passageway. She stopped in front of the room where they had met Samantha before with her attorney. She opened the door and motioned for them to step inside. Once they were inside, the bailiff walked in and faced them.

"In a minute, I'll bring Samantha in. I just wanted to let you know that I am praying for Samantha's success. She is way too young to be going to prison. I don't know her, but she's too young for that type of life." With that said, she walked to the far side of the room and walked out the other door. Shortly afterwards, the door reopened, and Samantha appeared.

Julie jumped up and moved toward Sam, holding her arms out to give Sam a hug. Sam avoided her and sat down on the closest chair with her head bowed. Julie was frozen in her tracks with an expression of pure shock. She first looked at Bill and then Clint, expecting an answer to *why*?

"Why are you acting like that? We just got you spared from prison," Clint said as he witnessed Julie's rejection.

Sam looked up at him with fire in her eyes. "Oh, the one who was never around, wondering why I feel like a throwaway child? Thinking I should bow down and give thanks to those who saved me?"

"Enough!" Bill quickly spoke. "We all made mistakes, and we all will share in the blame. That will not make it any easier in our situation. I think I can speak for us all in saying that we are glad it turned out the way it did. We now have to realize the changes that we all have to make, to learn from our mistakes and ensure they don't happen again. We all heard the rules that we will have to live by. It won't be easy, but it's a start of a new life to live by."

Julie, still shaken by her daughter's response, took a chair next to her. Julie looked at Clint, realizing that he had felt her pain. Julie gave a slight smile, turned, and looked at Sam.

"I wish you would understand how I hurt inside from hurting you. The thoughts of not being able to work on healing the suffering that you had lived. The amount of missing so much of your life, being so blind to it all. Being told that I cannot be with you or even talk to you for a year is almost more than I can bear. Please forgive me," Julie said as she bowed her head. Not many more words were spoken by her after that.

Within a few short minutes, there was a knock on the door. The door opened, and the bailiff returned.

"I have to take Samantha now. The court clerk asked that you all stop at her desk; she has some information for you all," the bailiff said as she motioned for Sam to get up and come with her.

Julie rose up to give Sam a hug, but Sam brushed her off and left with the bailiff. Julie collapsed back down in her chair, crying uncontrollably. Clint rose up and went by her side, and Bill had tears in his eyes also. They all gathered themselves and left for the court clerk's desk.

After walking down the long hallway, they entered through the door that read *Clerk of the Shawnee County Court*. Once inside the office, they walked up to the large wooden desk.

The lady looked up at them and said, "You must be with Samantha Roberts's family. Which one of you is Mr. Schyular?"

Bill raised his hand.

"Take these papers, and read over them. They explain what the judge has decreed on your part. You can take a seat over there if you like. You two must be Samantha's parents. Here are your papers. Read them carefully and then sign at the bottom of the last page. If you have any questions, feel free to ask."

Julie and Clint took the papers and a pen from the jar on her desk full of pens and pencils. They walked over to Bill and took a seat.

Julie gasped, "I can't believe that I can't see or even talk to her for a whole year."

Bill's stack of paperwork was more than twice the size of Julie's and Clint's. Clint sat motionless as he read through the paperwork. Julie kept wiping away the tears as her heart was breaking. She looked up at Bill to seek some comforting feelings from him. Bill finally looked at her with a smile. Feeling assured that everything was for the best, Julie signed the papers. Clint finished reading his paperwork and signed.

He looked over to Julie and said, "I've got to get going. Please keep me informed." He stood up, bent down, and kissed Julie.

She quickly stood up and embraced him. He turned around and handed back the paperwork to the court clerk. With that completed, he walked out.

Julie sat back down, the paperwork in her hand, and sat there wondering how all this would work out. Bill finally finished reading his paperwork and signed at the bottom of the last page. He himself was questioning if he could do it. He searched deep down in his heart, seeking answers from Sara. He was not sure what it was, but a feeling of peace came upon him.

Without a doubt, it was Sara saying, *I'm with you every step of the way.*

With this renewed feeling of self-assurance, Bill stood up over Julie and reached out to her. She stood up and saw in his face that everything would work out. A gentle peace came over her, a feeling she hadn't felt in years, now knowing that her father was there as he always had been.

They both walked over to the clerk's desk and handed her their paperwork. She took the paperwork and then handed Bill two sheets of paper.

"Here are the various phone numbers of departments that you will be working with. Social Services will be contacting you about the person who will be working with you. It'll probably be a couple of days before they get to you. If you have any questions about who to contact, please contact this office. That's my office number at the top. My name is Shirley. If there isn't anything else you need from me, have a good day," she said as she went back to attending to her work.

Julie and Bill left the office with Bill's arm around Julie's waist. They walked silently together down the hallway. Once outside, they walked over to Julie's car and looked at each other.

"Dad, do you need me to come over and help clean? I can take more time off work to help. I'm so sorry for not being there for you all these years. I don't know how I didn't understand how much you have done for me and the family all those years. I know now why mother loved you so much. Please forgive—"

Bill shook his head and said, "We learn life's lessons in different ways. Sometimes it's way past the time to know, but never too late to forgive." With that, he pulled her close to him and kissed her on the forehead. "It's time to start the next part of the journey. I need to get busy getting ready for a new roommate."

They both smiled at the thought.

Julie, with a smile on her face, got in her car and left. Bill, standing there, watched as she drove away, thinking to himself, *Hopefully she will understand the lessons she will learn from all of this.* Bill came back to reality and headed for his truck. Once he got inside, he reached for the glove box for a pencil and paper.

"Let's see, I'll need to get some paper towels, cleaning solutions, and bathroom cleaning stuff," he said out loud as he wrote them down. He set the pencil and paper down and started the truck. Within seconds, he was heading for the local grocery store. It wasn't long before he had all the things on the list and was heading home. The weather was nice, and the sky was blue. Soft white clouds were slowly passing through. As he drove, he hummed a joyful tune.

Pulling up to the house, Kipper was happily waiting for his best friend and wagging his tail in anticipation of the reunion. Bill got out of the truck with his arms full of the needed items for the house cleaning. Kipper just about knocked him down with the excitement of Bill's return. Bill was also thrilled to have such a welcome from Kipper. Once Bill was in the house, he set the bags of items on the kitchen table and turned to Kipper to give him a good petting. After the joyous reunion was over, Bill set about getting the house ready for Sam.

Two days later in the afternoon, the phone rang. Bill picked up the handset and spoke, "Hello."

The voice on the other end said, "Mr. Schyular, this is Wanda McDaniels from Kansas Social Services. I am calling to set up a time to come out and inspect your residence for acceptance of living accommodations. When would be a good time for this? Let's say in a week from now?"

Bill was caught off guard and said, "Yes, that would be fine. Next Tuesday? What time?"

Wanda responded, "How about 9:00 a.m. on Tuesday?"

He replied, "That would be fine. I'll be expecting you."

The following Tuesday morning, the sun was shining a blinding ray on Bill's sleeping eyes. Within moments, Bill was fully awake and thinking about the person who was coming to inspect the house. He figured he needed to get dressed, eat something, and then make another inspection of the house. As he took his stroll through rooms that he hadn't lived in since Sara left this world, a flood of memories from his past came to him. He realized that the house wasn't perfect but was presentable for any inspector. As he took a moment to look out the window, he came face-to-face with the reality that the yard was in shambles. Seeing that it was nearing 9 a.m., he knew it was too late to start the mower. Just as he thought maybe he could pick up some of the items lying in the yard, he spied the white SUV pulling into the driveway. His heart skipped a beat, and the lump in his throat had returned.

Bill thought it proper to go to the door and open it before they had time to ring the doorbell, which didn't work. Kipper, quick to welcome any newcomer to the farm, was quick to dart out the door. Kipper, with his tail wagging and excitement showing in his stride, was making his way to the SUV. As Bill stood in the open doorway, he watched as two people got out of the vehicle. The one driving was a middle-aged African American male, and the other was an older white female. The man stopped, took a look around the place, and patted Kipper on the head. The lady made no notion of her surroundings as she made her way up the sidewalk to the door. As she neared the door, Bill opened up the screen door and gave a smile.

"Mr. Schyular, I'm Wanda McDaniels, and my companion is Lionel Charles." She walked up to Bill and held out her hand. He took hold of her hand and gave a quick handshake.

"Good morning, Ms. McDaniels." He motioned for her to come into the house.

"Please call me Wanda." She stepped inside the house and Bill held the open screen door, waiting for Lionel. "Mr. Schyular, we are fully aware of your past years living by yourself. Our main concern is the sudden change of lifestyle with a sixteen-year-old, whom you just met for the first time in many years. Honesty, I think it will be too hard on you to bring a troubled teenager into your home and help her get back to a healthy lifestyle. I feel we are wasting our—"

Bill released the screen door and turned around to face Wanda. "Are you saying that it's a waste of time to help a child who has been in an environment that failed her? I was raised in a family that had to work hard to survive every day. I served my country in Vietnam, watching my friends die all around me. I married the woman of my dreams, raised two children of our own, and then buried the very same woman. There is nothing I haven't done, nothing that I cannot do, and by God's grace, I will not fail my granddaughter Samantha in her time of need."

By the time Bill had finished, Lionel had entered the house and was standing in the doorway with a look of total shock. Wanda was also taken back by the barrage of words coming from Bill's mouth. Bill took notice of their facial expressions and thought that maybe he should have toned it down a little. Lionel had walked by Bill and stood next to Wanda. His expression went from shock to nodding his head in approval.

Lionel spoke, "Mr. Schyular, my name is Lionel Charles, and I'm the Director of Children's Welfare for the county courts of Shawnee County. I felt your passion for your granddaughter. The main focus is to ensure you are fully aware of some of the problems that have happened in previous situations, such as yours. Wanda is here to look over your living conditions and make any suggestions that might be needed. If you don't mind, Wanda will do the inspection while we chat a while."

Bill nodded his head in agreement, turned, and closed the door.

Lionel spoke out again, "You seem to have a nice place here. How long have you lived here?"

This caught Bill off guard, and it took him a second to gather his thoughts through the endless years of memories. "All my life. Not for sure, but it's been a long time."

What Bill didn't realize was that Lionel was just trying to set Bill more at ease. Bill moved toward the front room, motioning for Lionel to go in and take a seat. Wanda had left and was making her tour of the house. Bill could hear her walking from one bedroom to another. Lionel got busy telling Bill about some problems that they'd had with elderly adults taking in teenagers. Within an hour, Lionel had finished up his talk and asked if Bill had any questions.

Bill was quick to say, "What rules will the court put on us for Samantha?"

"I was expecting you to ask that. Everyone always asks that one. You are supposed to know where she is at all times. You know, school, church, and the like. We can come at any time to check up on anything. We must receive copies of her school grades, attendance, and other outside activities that she gets involved in. We highly recommend that she get involved in sports, drama, band, or anything else that will provide a sense of belonging. We really don't want her to stay at home and not get involved. She will not be able to go to her parents' house without my approval—not even to pick up her clothes. We really don't want her to associate with any of her past friends; this could make her want to convert back. Other than that, not much else," he said with a wink. "When you sign the paperwork to get Samantha's release, there will be a few other things that you will have to adhere to."

Just as Bill and Lionel were finishing up their talk, Wanda came walking back into the room. Bill felt comfortable with Lionel, but now he was facing the biggest obstacle of the day, Wanda's inspection. She showed no emotion as she entered the room.

Lionel asked, "What do you have for Bill?"

Her reply was, "First off, I would like to apologize for what I said earlier. The court found that you were capable of raising Samantha, and I let my personal feelings get the best of me. Please forgive me. I can tell you have done a lot of house cleaning lately. I don't see anything that would prevent Samantha from living here. I still worry about a female teenager living with her—"

Lionel interrupted her and said, "I'll be assigning Cheryl Thomas as Samantha's caseworker, and she can assist Bill and Samantha on matters of female needs. Bill, Cheryl is a great person and can be a great benefit to the two of you. She can go shopping with Samantha and buy any clothes or items that she may need. If you are having any doubts about any problems that you are facing concerning a teenager, she has the knowledge and is a person who really cares."

Bill gave a huge sigh of relief, knowing that there would be things about a teenage girl that he wouldn't have a clue about. He also realized that Wanda was not happy about Lionel's opinion and that since she was no longer needed, she was ready to go.

Just as Lionel was standing up off the couch, Bill asked one last question, "When do I get to bring Samantha home?"

Lionel smiled and said, "Our reports will be on the judge's desk tomorrow morning, and as soon as she signs them, you'll be able to pick her up. I'll make sure that Cheryl will be present when you get Samantha, so the three of you will be able to meet."

Bill felt his heart swell and almost couldn't contain his emotions. Bill escorted them to the door and watched them get in the vehicle and drive down the driveway. Bill was full of excitement and couldn't wait to call Julie to tell her the good news. Just as he reached for the phone, he stopped and looked out the window. Emotions were stirring deep inside him, and he felt the desire to get on his knees and give thanks to the Lord. How long had it been since he'd felt this way? He fell to his knees with his hands clasped together; he searched deep down inside himself for words to pray. Within seconds, he was giving thanks for all that had transpired and asking for strength and wisdom for the coming days. Kipper came and laid down next to him, almost as if he were saying prayers too.

As he was just about to finish up praying, a thought came into his head: *Clothes; she doesn't have any clothes here to wear. Wow, I wasn't counting on that*, Bill thought to himself with a shocked look on his face. *I'd better give Julie a call; she will know everything that Sam will need.* With joy in his heart at passing this hurdle, he knew he needed to contact Julie and let her know the good news. Once back inside, he picked up the phone and dialed Julie's number. With a few rings, Julie answered.

"Hello, Julie. This is Dad," he said. "The house inspection went great, and now we have to wait till they release Sam. Also, I just found out we need to get Sam a complete new set of clothes. She can have nothing from her past while living with me. Can we meet and get the things she needs?"

"Oh, my God! That is awesome news," Julie answered excitedly. "Sure, let's go to the mall in Topeka. I'm sure we can find everything we need." Julie's voice was starting to break up and finally fell silent.

Bill could tell that Julie was breaking down and crying. With a short amount of small talk, they ended the call with, "I love you."

The next day, Bill and Julie met at the mall and left with everything Sam would need. The only talk was the anticipation of Sam being out of detention. By week's end, the long-awaited phone call came in.

"Mr. Schyular, this is Cheryl Thomas of the Kansas Department of Social Services. I am Samantha's caseworker and will be with her the whole time while she is on probation. I will be the one to contact in case of any emergencies or questions regarding Samantha. All the necessary paperwork is completed, and we can now release Samantha Roberts into your custody. Do you have the needed clothes and other items necessary for her?"

Bill replied, "Yes, I do."

"Then I would like to know the best time for you to come get her. You will need to bring a complete set of clothes for her. One last thing: I will need the names, addresses, and phone numbers of two adult females who will help with her. I'm sure you are knowledgeable about children, but being a man, there are things you might not know about young girls. You can bring the names in when you pick up Samantha. You can pick her up any time after today or as early as eight. The earlier the better."

"Tomorrow at eight is good for me," Bill said.

"Tomorrow at eight; please don't be late," Mrs. Thomas said.

Bill paused for a moment and then said, "I won't and thank you. See you tomorrow."

Bill hung up the phone and went to his favorite chair. Kipper led the way and waited for Bill to sit down before he laid on his blanket. Staring out the window, Bill closed his eyes, seeking an audience with his beloved Sara and wanting any type of guidance that she could provide him. Tears filled his eyes, and they began to slowly run down his cheeks.

He was asking questions such as, *Why now, why was I thrust into this situation? What meaning is to come from all this?* The time went by while he was searching his soul for unknown answers. It wasn't until Kipper laid his head on Bill's lap that Bill finally came back to life alone with Kipper.

After being in heavy thought for quite a while, Bill was starting to wonder what time it was. Looking at the clock on the mantel, he realized that it was getting late. He needed to feed Kipper and get Sam's items gathered up for tomorrow. He got up and let Kipper out of the back kitchen door while he fixed his dinner. Within minutes, Kipper was wanting to come back in and was awaiting dinner. Bill set about gathering her clothes, finding a bag to put them in, and checking and double-checking to make sure nothing was missing.

Then panic struck him. *What about the two names of adult women to help Sam?* He quickly went to the phone and called Mrs. Johnson. She answered the phone and would be glad to help in any way. She recommended that he call Tonya Martin, who had a kind heart and was well-known throughout the community. He finally found her phone number and gave her a call. Mr. Martin had answered the phone and would get her for him. Not too long later, Mrs. Martin was on the line. After a long discussion about Sam's situation, Mrs. Martin was thrilled to help. After getting all the necessary information for the required list, they ended their conversation. Everything was set for the next day's encounter for the start of a new life. Bill, being so consumed with all of this, went to bed without any dinner for himself.

With the sun beaming in his bedroom window, Bill awoke to a beautiful day. The birds were singing a cheerful song, and Bill thought to himself, *A great way to start a new beginning.* It was early enough that he didn't have to hurry. Putting a pot of coffee on and frying up some bacon, he set about getting himself presentable for the long-awaited encounter. Eating his breakfast and pouring a second cup of coffee, he sat back and pondered how Sara would have reacted to all of this. Kipper went to the back door, wanting out, so Bill got up and opened the screen door to let him out. After sitting back down to finish off his coffee, the phone rang. It was Julie, and by the tone of her voice, she was worrying herself sick over Sam coming to live with him. The questions were flying fast, one right after another. He couldn't get a word in edgewise. He finally calmed her down by convincing her that everything was set and there was nothing to worry about. He finally ended the conversation by saying it was time to go. After hanging up the phone, he got the bag with Sam's items, checked his pockets for his wallet and keys, and away he went.

Walking out the back door, he stopped and petted Kipper and told him, "Be a good boy and be ready for our new roommate. I'll be back soon."

Kipper followed him out to the truck and stood as Bill got in. Once the engine of the truck started, Kipper knew he was leaving and headed back to the porch to watch him drive away. It wasn't long before the truck was out of sight. On the way, Bill's thoughts were buzzing with all the different ways to greet Sam. He wanted to start off on the right foot and not offend her or her caseworker. With so many thoughts running through his head, he found that he was already at the place to meet with Sam. It was 7:47 a.m., and timing was going as planned. He found a parking spot in front and close to the front door. Things couldn't have gone better. After shutting off the truck, he sat and pondered how everything would go with the meeting. With his eyes closed, he sought one last moment for Sara's advice. A feeling of peace came over him, and he got out of the truck and headed in.

He walked through the front doors and went up to the front counter, where several people were. One lady smiled and asked if she could help him.

"I'm Bill Schyular, and I'm here to pick up Samantha Roberts," he said as he looked around.

"Who is the caseworker for Ms. Roberts?" the lady asked.

"Mrs. Thomas," Bill replied.

"Oh, yeah, I'll get her for you," the lady said as she picked up the phone and called. When she hung up, she said, "She will be right with you. You can have a seat over there."

Within minutes, Mrs. Thomas came through the large door to Bill's right. As she came up to Bill, she smiled and held her hand out. Bill stood up and shook her hand.

"I'm Cheryl Thomas. Mr. Schyular, I'm glad to see you are on time. We don't always have people show up when they are supposed to. Samantha is in the back, waiting for her clothes. Once she gets changed and you sign some paperwork, you two can be on your way. Let me take her clothes back to her, and I'll be back to go over the paperwork." With that said, she took the bag and left. It wasn't long before she returned with a clipboard with papers on it.

They both walked over to a small table close to the wall. After they were seated, she started in with, "Mr. Schyular, I assumed that you are aware that I will be in contact with you at least twice a week. More than likely, I'll be coming to your house to check on Samantha and your house. If things are working out, maybe only once a week, and could be by phone. Do you have the list of two adult women who will be helping you with Samantha?"

Bill handed her the list.

"Thank you. Do you have any questions for me? Let me first say that Samantha is very confused about all that's going on. One more thing: she needs to write a journal every day. She doesn't have to write about what she's done that day; it would be best if she would write out her feelings. Hopefully, this will release some of the frustrations that she has bottled up inside. It would also be something that I could read and have a better knowledge of what's going on inside her. Let's hope it goes well for her."

Bill nodded his head in agreement. He finished signing the paperwork, and Mrs. Thomas got up and went to get Sam.

Soon she came back with Sam behind her. The expression on Sam's face was one of lifeless sorrow. As she got closer to Bill, she bowed her head and refused to look at him. Bill thought to himself, *This can't be a good way to start off.*

Mrs. Thomas walked over to Bill and said, "She's not crazy about the clothes, but I guess it really doesn't matter, does it? I'll call you tomorrow morning to see how the night went. Samantha, please try to understand that we are only trying to help you. Don't give in to negative thoughts; things will get brighter for you. I'll be seeing you in the next couple of days. Goodbye!"

With that said, Bill led Sam out the door and to his truck. Still refusing to look Bill in the eyes, she reluctantly got in.

When Bill got in, he looked over at her. "Please fasten your seatbelt."

"Why?" Sam snapped back.

"Because this truck is going nowhere until it is. Plus, I told you to!" Bill said in a stern voice.

She buckled up her seatbelt. Bill started up the truck and pulled away from the curb. The whole time he was driving home, he searched his mind to think of something to say. Sam kept her hands folded in her lap and gazed out the window.

CHAPTER 6

LEARNING TO COPE

It was late afternoon when Bill and Sam got home. He brought the truck to a stop and shut off the engine. He took a glance over at Sam and realized he couldn't think of a thing to say. Sam sat there leaning on the door, her hands folded together between her knees. Her head was bowed down, and her hair covered her face. She sat there as still as a statue.

Bill finally spoke, "Sam, let's go inside, and I'll find something for dinner."

"I'm not hungry," came the voice from beneath the hair. "Just leave me alone!"

"I will not tolerate that tone of voice from you," Bill said in a voice that he hadn't used in twenty years. "Life has dealt us both a situation that neither of us asked for."

Sam lifted her head and glared at Bill. Then she spoke with total defiance, "Why don't you take me back and let me rot in jail? Nobody else wants to deal with me! That would end your bad situation!"

Bill, taken aback by this attitude, thought of firing back, but words from Sara came to him. *Teaching love does not come from words of hatred. Love has to be given from a heart that cares. Do not let hatred rule your words.*

With a tear in his eye, Bill spoke, "Sam, I care what happens to you. Let me help you in any way I can. We are both at a disadvantage in this relationship. Please, let's go into the house. I have someone I would like for you to meet." He knew Kipper might help break some of the hatred that Sam was harboring.

Bill opened his door and got out. He walked around the truck to Sam's side and motioned for her to come on out. With hesitation, Sam opened her door and stepped out. She stopped and surveyed the location of her new residence. Her face was in total shock.

"I'm living on a farm! You've got to be kidding me! When I was told you live out in the country, I didn't realize you lived with cows and chickens." She shook her head in disbelief and gave Bill a look of hatred.

Bill took a deep breath, turned, and walked into the house. He hadn't taken into account that Sam might not have known of his living existence. At least he knew that she didn't have a clue how to get out of here.

Kipper had been waiting anxiously at the back door. When Bill came in, Kipper went out to meet the new guest.

As Kipper was excitedly dancing around Sam, all she could do was pull her arms up next to her and scream, "Get away!"

This didn't stop Kipper's excitement.

Bill walked back out onto the porch and said, "This is Kipper, and he is so excited to meet you. He won't bite and is a very loving dog."

She replied, "Make him stop. I don't like dogs."

"Come on, Kipper. She doesn't know you yet," Bill said as Kipper came bouncing back to him to show him his affection for returning.

Bill turned and opened the door for Kipper, and they both walked in, closing the door behind them. As Bill was rummaging through the refrigerator for dinner, Sam slowly came in. She scanned the surroundings as she walked through the kitchen. She made her way into the dining room and then the front room. Bill could tell she found the bathroom, for he heard the door close and lock. He continued on his quest for a late-night dinner. He pulled out some bacon and eggs and thought they would be as good as anything else. With the skillet heating up, he went about setting the table. Kipper was following Bill around, hoping he would set a place for him at the table. After several minutes, Sam reappeared at the kitchen door.

"Where am I supposed to sleep?" Sam asked in a defiant tone.

"Here, I'll show you." Bill moved past her. Coming to the hallway, he pointed down to the bedroom next to the bathroom. "That will be your bedroom, and this is your bathroom. I have a bathroom off of my bedroom. I expect you to keep both of them clean and your dirty laundry picked up. We got you a whole new set of clothes; if you need anything else, let me know. I'll have dinner ready in a few minutes."

"I told you I'm not hungry," she said as she went into the bedroom.

"Suit yourself, but it'll be at the table when you are ready. If Kipper doesn't get it first." Bill said this with a smile on his face. Bill returned to the kitchen with Kipper by his side. He flipped the bacon over and thought to himself, *She's got to be hungry; she hasn't eaten all day.* With the bacon done, he placed it on a paper towel on a plate and commenced cracking eggs. Dropping several in the skillet, he went over to the refrigerator and pulled out the gallon jug of fresh milk. Pouring himself a tall glass, he quickly returned to the stove and tended to his eggs. With both the bacon and eggs done, he sat himself down and ate. As he was finishing up his meal, Sam reappeared at the kitchen door.

"Here, sit down and I'll cook some eggs to go along with the bacon," Bill said as he got up. "How do you like your eggs?"

Sam just came in and sat down without speaking.

Bill responded with, "Okay, scrambled it is." He reheated the skillet and pulled two eggs out of the refrigerator. Looking over at her, he couldn't understand how she could be just a shell of a girl at her young age. Within minutes, the eggs were done, and he scooped them up and set them on her plate. He then passed the plate of bacon over to her. He then went back and sat down, watching her as she devoured her meal. This whole time, Kipper was on guard duty for any food that came off the table. Normally, nothing hit the floor because he caught it in midflight.

With the meal gone, Bill could sense Sam was more at ease than before.

He slowly spoke, "If you want to take a shower, you will find your clothes in the dresser and other items hanging up in the closet. There is a robe hanging behind the door of the bedroom. I'm going to do the dishes and then take Kipper outside. If you need anything, just let me know."

Sam slowly lifted her head and gave a slight nod. She got up and went into the other room. He got up and cleared the table, as Kipper was looking for anything leftover for him. With the dishes done and Kipper disappointed by the lack of scraps, both of them went outside for the evening stroll around the yard.

The new day dawned, and the sun was up bright and early. Bill arose wondering how the day would go. It was after six when he got to the kitchen and put on a pot of coffee. He glanced over at the calendar and realized it was Wednesday, June the third. It was a special day for Bill—it was Sara's birthday. He filled his mind with nothing but Sara.

For the moment, he did not think of Sam. His heart was full of joy with thoughts of her. Even though he still missed her, he had a new mission in life, and it would have been hers also. With so many happy thoughts, he lost all sense of time. When he came back to reality, he was sitting in his chair in the front room. He returned to the kitchen and poured himself a cup of coffee. He retrieved the bacon and some eggs and began to remake the dinner he had the night before. The aroma must have awakened Sam, for she appeared once again in the doorway. He was surprised to see her up so early, but then he saw that it was almost eight.

The plates were full of scrambled eggs and bacon, and without hesitation, both were eating. Kipper once again kept his eyes peeled for anything that dropped. The scraping of the forks across the plates told Kipper that breakfast was over. Sam got up and was walking out of the kitchen when Bill spoke.

"Your turn to do the dishes. I did them last night. We will take turns doing them."

"I don't do dishes!" she snapped back.

"You do them now," he quickly responded. "This is not a free ride for you to do what you want."

She turned around and gave him a look of total disgust. She paused for a few moments and said, "Fine, you'll get what you ask for!"

"I'll get them done right, or you'll keep doing them till you get them right," Bill said as he stared her in her eyes. "It starts right now that you earn your keep. After the dishes are done, I'll show you how to feed the chickens and cows."

Sam just rolled her eyes and sat back down on her chair. Mumbling something under her breath, Bill just let it go. Kipper, sensing something was amiss, went over to Sam and gave a quiet growl. He just wanted for Sam to take notice of him; she spun away from him. Not to be rejected, he just jumped around her chair, coming face to face with her. This just seemed to infuriate Sam even more.

Bill, taking notice of the situation, spoke, "He just wants to be friends with you. He's the best friend you'll ever have. Give him a chance."

"I told you I don't like dogs!" Sam yelled back.

"First off, don't ever talk to me like that!" Bill demanded. "Don't ever mistreat him. He doesn't deserve that. But you might want to be careful; he might just grow on you."

Sam straightened out in her chair and stared at Bill. He thought, *At least she didn't have anything to come back with.*

"Dish soap is under the sink. Make sure you wipe down the table and kitchen tops. Once you wash the skillet, wipe it dry with a paper towel and set it back on the stove. I'll be in the garden when you get done, come find me. Any questions?"

After Bill had spoken, he and Kipper went out the back door. When the screen door slammed shut, Sam jumped.

As Bill and Kipper were walking toward the garden, Bill said to Kipper, "Wonder how long it'll take her to do the dishes? Keep working on her. If anybody can change her, it's you." Bill grabbed a hoe from the small tool shed and commenced weeding around the garden. Kipper was busy looking for squirrels to chase. Most of them were yelling obscenities at him from a safe branch. Finally, Kipper gave up and found one of his chew toys, picked it up, and went over in the shade to chew on it.

It was over an hour until she showed up at the garden. Without looking up, Bill said, "Come on over here, and I'll let you hoe the weeds out of the garden."

Sam tilted her head back and rolled her eyes.

"This row is green beans, and that one over there is sweet peas. You only hoe out the weeds in between. It's not hard to do, but do pay attention that you're not taking out the vegetables."

Sam drudgingly walked over and took the hoe.

Sam and Bill worked in the garden for over an hour. He then showed her how to feed the cows and chickens. Sam was afraid of the cows at first but then took kindly to them. The day flew by, and after having dinner, she went to her room and locked the door. Bill thought to himself, *Not a bad day.*

Bill came to her door and softly knocked. "Sam, I got you a pen and table. Mrs. Thomas wants you to write a journal every day. She doesn't necessarily want what you did today but would like for you to write down some of the feelings that you're feeling."

There was a short silence, and then Sam said, "What I'm feeling right now is not what anyone wants to read about."

"It doesn't matter what you write about, but maybe it will release some frustration that you are harboring. Please open your door and get these," he spoke as he hoped she would be more responsive to things that might help her out.

Sam was inside her room, lying on the bed, wondering how much more she could take. She hesitated for a moment, then reluctantly opened the door and took the pen and tablet. She gave a look at him as if to say, *Why don't you just leave me alone?* She closed the door and went back to her bed. Throwing the tablet and pen on the dresser drawer, she thought to herself, *Like hell I'll journal!*

Within a short while, she heard scratching at the door and a low whining sound. She got up and opened the door. There was Kipper with a tennis ball in his mouth. Kipper, tail wagging, dropped the ball, and it bounced inside her room.

Sam said, "Go away and take your ball with you." She picked up the ball and tossed it into the hallway. Kipper, in a spirit of pure joy, chased after it. Sam closed the door. Once again, she heard the scratching and whining sounds. When she opened the door, Kipper was ready to chase the ball. This time, he darted past her and spun around with a look of, *Take the ball if you can.*

"Ugh!" was all Sam could say. She closed the door, went back, and laid on her bed. Kipper, not to be ignored, jumped back and forth in front of her. Finally, he dropped the ball and laid down on the rug next to her bed. Nighttime fell, and they were both asleep.

When the early morning light appeared, Bill was busy getting breakfast ready. He then realized that Kipper wasn't around. He searched throughout the house, and Kipper was nowhere to be found. Bill wondered if he left him outside. He took a quick look, but Kipper was not to be seen. With the aroma of breakfast being cooked, Sam awoke to find Kipper lying next to her in bed. She looked at him in amazement and wondered how he got there without waking her. She slid her legs over to the side of the bed. Oh, how her body's muscles ached from yesterday. She thought to herself, *I don't even think I can walk.* Bill could hear Sam moving into the bathroom, and about that time, Kipper came bouncing into the kitchen.

"So that's where you've been," Bill said with a slight chuckle. "Good boy. Keep working on her. She needs a good friend."

Within minutes, Sam entered the kitchen and began walking as if none of her legs worked. She slowly walked over to her chair and fell down upon it.

"Little sore this morning?" Bill said as he flipped the pancakes over. "Don't worry; your body will soon get used to manual labor." He then slid two pancakes on a plate, along with bacon and a couple of eggs.

CAPTAIN MCDOOGLE

Placing it on the table in front of her, he looked for some sign of life from her. "We need to mow the yard and trim up some trees this morning. Some of their branches are hanging low. After breakfast, if you've got any dirty laundry, go ahead and get them in the washer. I'll do up the dishes, and then we can start on the yard."

Sam just looked up at him and rolled her eyes. She thought to herself, *How can I do anything the way my body feels?*

Bill finished up the dishes and, with Kipper by his side, went out to the one-car garage and pulled out the mower. He checked the oil and filled it with gas. With two pulls of the starter cable, it took off running. He thought, *Where is Sam?* He walked back into the house and found Sam still sitting in the kitchen chair. "Come on, up and at 'em," Bill said with a half-hearted grin. "Go get your laundry in the washer, and then come on out to the yard. Daylight is a-burning."

Sam looked at him with a totally blank look. Finally making it to her feet, she slowly made her way back to her bedroom. Bill just shook his head as he watched her leave the room.

It took Sam over fifteen minutes to finally make it out to the yard, where Bill and Kipper were waiting. It seemed to Bill that it almost took her that long just to get close to the mower. Sam stopped short and looked at Bill with a disgusted face. With a full explanation of the operation of the mower, she took hold of it and was off and running. It wasn't long before she had wiped out half of the flowerbeds and threw rocks all over the place when she got too near the driveway. She just kept on going, not checking to see if he was watching. Kipper, sensing she was a rookie at mowing, kept his distance far beyond her. While she mowed, Bill got the weed trimmer and trimmed the remaining parts that couldn't be mowed. With the yard mowed, she pulled the mower up next to Bill and walked away from it. She headed back into the house and to her room. Kipper, sensing the danger was over, happily followed her.

As Bill was putting away the equipment, he noticed a blue SUV pulling into the driveway. When it pulled up to the house, Cheryl Thomas emerged from the SUV.

"Good morning, Mr. Schyular. I hope I caught you at a good time?" she said as she walked up to him.

"I'd say just about perfect timing," Bill said as he wiped his hands of any dirt or grease. "Sam and I just finished mowing the yard."

"Did Sam help mow?" she said in a surprised tone of voice.

"Yep, she did all of the mowing, to include the flower beds and part of the driveway," he said with a chuckle. "She's in the house; more than likely, in her room. Go on in. She's in there somewhere."

"I will in a minute. I need to know from you how she's been acting," she said.

"She doesn't say anything to give me a clue as to what she's feeling. She does do what I ask of her, but it's been a quiet start to a relationship. I'm hoping Kipper will break her silence."

"Well, sounds like it's a start," she said as she smiled at him. She turned and headed into the house. She walked slowly through the house, checking for any signs of Sam. She finally got to Sam's bedroom door and gently knocked.

A harsh-sounding voice cried out, "Who is it?"

"It is Cheryl Thomas; I've come to talk to you. Can I come in?"

Cheryl could hear footsteps and the unlocking of the door. Sam opened the door and gave Cheryl a look of total discontentment. Sam stepped back away and motioned for her to come in. Kipper was standing behind Sam, who was having a hard time trying to control himself with a new visitor. As Cheryl entered the room, Kipper was ready to greet her. She petted him for a second and then looked around the room.

Cheryl then spoke, "How's it been going? I heard you mowed the yard this morning."

"Yeah, and I hoed the garden, fed cows and chickens, did the dishes, and I'm dealing with this dog!" Sam snapped back.

"Honey, it's all part of life," Cheryl said in a soft voice. "Life sometimes brings to us things that we don't want to do but have to do. This dog seems to be very friendly and only wants to be loved. I really don't think that he's going to be any type of burden on you."

"His name is Kipper, and he won't leave me alone." Sam spoke as she sat down on the bed. "I wake in the morning and wonder what else I'll have to do."

"Have you given it any thought about doing summer school to earn enough credits to finish your sophomore year of school, so you won't have to do it all over again? It would really look good to the courts if you would," Cheryl asked.

Sam looked up at her with a puzzled look. "Hadn't thought about that. How do you think ol' farmer John would take to that idea?"

"That ol' farmer John is your grandfather, and he has taken on a lot and needs to be shown a little more respect from you. He hasn't done anything but try to help you learn the ways of life. I'm sure he will do anything he can to help you make it through all this. I'll talk to him and find out if we can get you to complete the necessary credits so you can attend your Junior year of school. Promise me that you'll try to see the value in all that we are doing for you. I will leave you now and will be calling on you in the next couple of days. Goodbye!"

With that said, Sam just raised her hand in a farewell gesture as Ms. Thomas walked out the door.

When Cheryl reached the kitchen, she found Bill there, drinking a cup of coffee at the table. "Well, how did it go?" he said as he took another sip. "Will you join me and have a cup of coffee?"

"Quite well, I think," she said as she sat down at the table. "Yes, please. Do you have any sugar and cream? I'm so glad that you are keeping her busy. It keeps her mind off of her situation and helps her earn her keep."

"Sure do," Bill said as he got up and poured her a cup. He pulled out the cream from the refrigerator and put the sugar bowl on the table. He then fetched a spoon from the silverware drawer. "She hasn't been given a life's lesson in responsibility."

"I mentioned to Samantha about attending summer school to complete her credits to finish up her Sophomore year of high school. I will check out all the available classes for her to take." she said as she poured some creamer into her coffee and added a spoonful of sugar. "It will have to be in Topeka, would that be a problem?"

"Not if she completes it," he said as he took another drink of coffee. "Do you think she'll do it?"

"I think she will, but it will take you away from the farm," she replied as she looked up at him.

"When it comes to Sam, the farm can wait. I can do everything that needs to be done before we leave for the day," Bill proclaimed.

"Okay, I will find out everything that I can and get back to you," Cheryl said.

With a small amount of chatter, Cheryl and Bill concluded their conversation and coffee. She quickly left, and Bill was cleaning up the table and doing the dishes. Kipper came bouncing in, and Bill was glad to give him some attention. Bill thought to himself, *I need to get the car running. Can't drive the truck all the time.* He headed out the back door, with Kipper leading the way. Kipper took off to get his chew toy and settled down in the shade of the old oak tree. Bill opened the garage door and stared at the neglected car, covered in dust. He first started to unload the various boxes of useless junk piled on the car's hood and trunk. He jumped in the driver's seat and tried to start it, but as he suspected, the battery was dead. Upon opening the hood, he noticed that the battery terminals were highly corroded and needed to be cleaned. After that task was completed, he put the battery charger on it and walked back into the house.

Within a few days, Cheryl called Bill and let him know of a private school for young people in the same situation as Sam. They would evaluate Sam's school credits and set up courses that would fulfill her requirements for completion of her high school sophomore year. The classes would start at 8:00 a.m. and end at noon, Monday through Thursday, for eight weeks. The cost was estimated to be around $1,200. Bill told her that would be acceptable. He would contact Julie and Clint, and they could share in the cost. He called Julie, and she said that would be great. She would let Clint know and pay the cost.

Sam was enrolled in the school, and Bill would hang around until classes were over. Sam seemed to be a little more at ease, probably with the escape from the farm and being able to communicate with other students. Weeks went by fast, and then the final day of testing was completed. It would be several days before the results were handed out. Sam was overjoyed that the classes were complete, and her relationship with Kipper developed into a budding friendship. Sam and Kipper were almost constant companions. Bill was almost jealous of the fact that Kipper was spending more time with her than him. He knew that Kipper was doing the right thing and wouldn't want to see it any other way.

It was early August when the results of Sam's schooling were released. She completed the classes with a combined total of eighty percent. She had fulfilled the requirements to enter her junior year of high school. But the one main obstacle she had to overcome was her relationship with her grandfather. During the two and a half months that Sam was living with him, she had only spoken a few words. None of them showed any type of kindness. This was really starting to weigh heavily on Bill's mind. He knew in a very short time she would be entering the local high school, and there would be another problem: *boys!*

Bill realized that it was the right time to have that sit-down talk with Sam and try to clear the air with her. He dreaded the thought of her falling back into her shell, but he knew it had to happen. He went to her bedroom door and knocked.

"Sam, I want you to come out to the front room and have a talk."

She replied, "Talk about what?"

"Us," he spoke in a soft tone.

Again, she spoke, "What about us?"

"Please just come out, and we can figure out how our lives will be in the upcoming months," Bill said with a lump in his throat. He could hear her walking across her room and unlocking the door.

As she opened the door, Kipper came walking out, with Sam following behind. She didn't even give Bill a glance as she walked past him. She went into the front room and sat in Sara's chair, with Kipper lying down next to her. As Bill entered the room, he thought to himself, *Maybe Sara would be holding her in her arms while sitting in that chair.* Bill walked over to his chair and sat down.

While staring out the window, he softly spoke, "Sam, you have done amazingly well since you have been here. You have done everything that I asked of you. You started and completed the schoolwork to finish off your sophomore year of school. You kept your room and clothes clean without having to be told to. Ms. Thomas has given you rave reviews to the courts. The thing that bothers me the most is our relationship. I don't think that I've been unfair in my treatment of you. So, why is it that you find it hard to open up to me?"

Sam looked up at him and, for the first time, gave him a look of understanding. "I guess it's because I didn't know you. That you would treat me as a throwaway child and really didn't want anything to do with me. That I was forced upon you. At first, when you made me do the chores, I thought I was only here to be your slave. I've never had anyone take the time to show me how to do things. I was always on my own to learn things and do things for myself. Why have you been such a mystery to me? Why wouldn't my mother let me see you?

Bill looked at her with a tear in his eye and said, "I guess there are lots of reasons. Mainly, I was always working and didn't spend any time with her and Justin. I haven't seen Justin since he graduated from high school. Since I didn't spend time with them, they don't want to spend time with me. Your grandmother understood, but your mother and Justin didn't." Bill stopped and stared out the window, not knowing what else to say.

"So, I guess they didn't really know you," Sam said as she watched him sit there motionless. "Since Grandma died, you have been all alone." Sam felt the same heartache that he had felt for so many years. Tears were swelling up in her eyes at the thought that the two of them were both alone.

Bill turned and looked at Sam. Tears were now streaming down both their faces.

"For all the years since your grandma passed, I prayed to the Lord Almighty to take me away from this world and let me return to Sara.

Kipper has given me a reason to stay, and now with you, I have purpose. I feel like your grandma has guided us to be together. Not to live life alone. You are my purpose in life. I will not let you down. Things will only get better if you trust me. I will not lead you astray."

Sam wiped the tears from her eyes and said, "Grandfather, if you help me, I will do what you ask of me." She then jumped up, ran over to him, and gave him a sincere hug as if to never let him go. She buried her head in his shoulder, feeling a feeling that she had never felt before.

A rush of feelings encompassed Bill's body that he hadn't felt since Sara last hugged him. He reached around her and returned the embrace. For several minutes, tears were streaming from the two of them. They both felt a sense of fulfillment. Kipper couldn't contain himself and jumped up to be part of the moment.

Neither one of them wanted the moment to end, so they finally pulled themselves apart and gathered their thoughts. Kipper was jumping around both of them, knowing that things were the way they should be. Both, with red eyes from crying, looked at each other and gave a short laugh. Sam went back to her chair, and Bill turned in his chair and faced Sam.

Bill spoke first, "There's a lot we need to share with each other. I know so little about you, and I'm sure the same is true for you about me. Your grandmother was my life. I treasured the ground she walked on. My purpose was to ensure that she would never be sad or without. When Justin came along, we were family and had another mouth to feed. I had to take on every job that I could. It was tough trying to make ends meet. Then your mother came into our lives. Your grandmother was so happy. A boy for me and a girl for her. I failed in that department, not realizing my responsibility to be a father to both of my children.

When she saw him looking at her, she said, "Why has it taken so long for us to meet? Wasn't I worth seeking out?" she asked with a slight quiver in her voice. Her eyes were reaching out to him for an answer he knew he would have to face.

He took a large swallow and said, "My failures are my own. These are the past lessons that I'm trying to learn from. They come from a lack of understanding of the needs of life. When I found out that you were born, I had been placed in my own miserable life and sheltered from any family life that I knew. I knew your mother really didn't want me around, so I kept myself tucked away from everyone else. Was I wrong? Yes, I know that now. I failed you, your mother, and your Uncle Justin. Give me a chance to learn from my past failures, and hopefully I can regain my self-worth to you."

Sam came closer to Bill and said, "Let's both work on our past failures together, and maybe we can live our lives right." Bill nodded his head in agreement.

Bill stood up and started for the back door, then he stopped and looked back at her and said, "I think it's time for some excitement in our lives."

She got up and followed him outside. He motioned for her to go to the old green Chevy pickup truck sitting by the garage. Sam climbed in on the passenger side, while Bill took a second to look around the yard. He was realizing that what mattered most was the God-given chance to make a difference in their lives. He felt excitement growing inside his heart.

With a quick turn of the key, the old engine fired up, and they were on their way down the long driveway. It was early evening, and the sun was still bright and hot. Since the truck had no air conditioning, the windows were rolled down, and both were choking on the dust from the gravel road. It wasn't long before he wheeled up to Alma's pizza parlor.

When he shut off the truck, he turned to her and said, "I think it's about time you get your driver's license."

Her face lit up like a Christmas tree.

With a smile that went from ear to ear, her only reply was, "Really?"

He nodded his head in agreement, and then they both got out and headed in for pizza.

Bill was realizing that Sam had come back as a happy young lady. Things had taken the turn that he hoped for. He paused for a moment, closed his eyes, and gave thanks to Sara for leading him down this path and for giving him reason to live and a chance to correct some of the wrongs of life. As they ordered the baked delight, both had their arms around each other. It was a feeling that he hadn't felt since Sara left. It was a great feeling; one he wouldn't take for granted again.

CHAPTER 7

A LIFE TO LIVE

With their bellies full, Sam and Bill headed out the door, arms reaching for each other. Reaching the truck, Sam paused for a moment and looked at him. "When do you think I can get my driver's license?"

"Well, first I have to check with the courts. Then we will need to find a driving school that can issue a driver's license. I'll check tomorrow to find out, is that okay?" Bill said as he wondered if the court would allow it.

With that said, they both jumped in the beat-up truck and headed for home. Kipper was overly excited about their return, and it took him quite a while to settle into the nightly slumber.

The next morning, Bill found himself the last to awaken. Sam and Kipper were out playing in the yard. The sun was out bright, and the birds' singing was so pleasing to the ears. Bill set about preparing breakfast and thought to himself, *Maybe I shouldn't have said anything about the driver's license till I checked with the courts. If they won't allow it, this could send Sam back into silence.* With the breakfast meal done, he went to the back door and called them in. With the sound of Sam's laughter and Kipper's barking, he could tell that pure joy was happening in the yard. Sam and Kipper entered the kitchen, acting like there was not a care in the world. With the completion of the meal, Sam gave notice that she was doing the dishes, which totally caught Bill off guard.

It was later in the morning and Sam was out in the yard with Kipper when Bill reached for the phone. Within seconds, he was in contact with Mrs. Thomas. After explaining his thought of letting Sam get her driver's license, Mrs. Thomas was pondering the thought.

She hesitated for a moment and then said, "If we can ensure that she is able to drive and that she wouldn't return to her home and try and settle back into the life that she had."

Bill's reply was, "I will have control of the keys to the vehicles. She has opened up to me and seems to be happy in her situation. Can you come out tomorrow and talk with her about this? I think she deserves a chance at this."

"Sure, I can be there around nine o'clock. By the way, have you got her enrolled in school yet?" Mrs. Thomas asked.

"Enrollment starts Monday," Bill said. "I'll ensure she will have the needed supplies for school. I was wondering if you could take her shopping and buy her some new clothes for school? Of course, I'll pay for everything, even lunch."

"I'll have to check my schedule, but I'm sure we can work something out. Let's see how tomorrow goes before I approach the courts about her driver's license. Thanks for calling. Have a nice day."

"Thanks for all you do, and goodbye!" Bill hung up the phone and thought to himself, *I hope this all works out.*

The next day brought a bright and sunny morning. Bill got up early and fixed his morning coffee. As he sat at the kitchen table, he pondered thoughts of how Sam had come back to reality, and Kipper was mostly the reason why. He missed the morning walks with Kipper, but he has done a greater deed with Sam. He started to think about Mrs. Thomas coming and taking Sam shopping. *Hopefully,* he thought, *she will find Sam responsible enough to have a driver's license.* He heard the sounds of the coffee percolating in the coffee pot, so he got up and poured a cup. He grabbed the cup and headed out the back door. As he slowly walked along the sidewalk leading to the driveway, he had a vision of Sara walking toward him with a smile on her face. A tear slowly slid down his face, knowing that she was with him all the time. As he sipped the hot brew, it was as if he could once again gaze into her eyes. The moment was gone with the opening of the back door, and Kipper was racing to be by his side. Sam was walking out the door too, and Kipper was walking up to Bill.

"Well, Grandpa! What's on the agenda for today?" she said as she stood by his side.

"Mrs. Thomas is coming to take you shopping for school clothes. She should be here by ten o'clock, so we better get some breakfast down your throat and clean up the house," Bill said with a wink of the eye.

"Really, I will be able to pick out my own clothes? Oh, my God, I was wondering what I was going to wear to school! This is so cool!" Sam jumped into Bill's arms, making him spill the remaining coffee in his cup. Kipper was part of the act as he was jumping around them, barking from all the excitement.

"Okay, enough of the silliness. Let's get moving so we will be ready for her." Bill said as he shook the spilled coffee off his hand.

Sam ran back into the house, with Kipper hot on her trail. Bill slowly made his way back to the house, searching for the vision of Sara that he had before. His heart swelled, knowing that Sam was in the position that they all wanted her to be in. He thought that he should give Julie a call and update her on all that had happened. He reached the kitchen and started whipping up some pancake batter. With some bacon and eggs to add to them, it would fill their bellies for a good day of shopping.

By the time the food was placed on the table, Sam was sitting down and ready to eat.

Sam started the conversation first. "When can I start my driver's license course?"

"I talked to Mrs. Thomas about it yesterday. She said that she would talk to the courts about it. We have to have the court's permission for you to have one. Sam, I want you to know how proud of you I am. Things didn't start out too well when you were first released. I feel that you have adjusted well to the living situation that you're in. You have completed the necessary courses so you can go into your junior year of high school. You have proven that you are working toward a better you, and I feel you could be trusted with a driver's license. But remember, you are on a serious type of probation, and the court decides what you can and cannot do. You have another nine months until you can see or speak to your mother. They especially don't want you to reconnect with your old friends."

Sam's smile faded from her face. Bill could see a tear running down her cheek. Even Kipper sensed Sam's sadness and laid his head in her lap.

Sam looked up and said, "I understand."

"Talk to Mrs. Thomas today about it. Give her the confidence that she needs to feel you are ready for the driver's license." Bill said, nodded his head in agreement. This brought a slight smile to Sam's face.

With breakfast over, Bill set about cleaning up the kitchen and dishes while Sam was busy getting ready for the day's shopping. Mrs. Thomas arrived at the house at 10:15 a.m., and Kipper was there to greet her. Both Bill and Sam walked out together and walked up to her.

"Here she is! She's ready for the day," Bill said as he handed Mrs. Thomas $300. "Make sure you have lunch too! If you spend more, just let me know."

"Oh my! Aren't you coming along too?" Mrs. Thomas proclaimed.

"Nope, I feel that's a woman thing!" Bill said as he winked at Sam.

Nothing more had to be said; the two ladies of the day were off and running. Bill and Kipper watched as the SUV slowly drove down the driveway and long out of sight.

He looked down at Kipper and said, "Let's take a walk down by the pond. We hadn't had a chance to do that in a while."

Kipper knew the way, and the two of them walked to the gate in the fence and passed through it. Kipper was leading the way, taking time to take a quick sniff at various places. As they walked down the path, they kicked up a rabbit, but Kipper wasn't in the mood to give chase. He was enjoying the shared time with Bill. It was a relaxing time, walking around the pond and giving Bill a chance to skip some rocks across the pond. He got six skips, which was his best throw. Bill remembered days like this in his youth. Oh, how he missed his family. Then, once again, he had a vision of Sara in the distance with a smile on her face. It was as if to remind him that she was always with him.

They returned to the house, and Bill decided to get the old car going again. If Sam did get her driver's license, she would need a vehicle to drive. But first, he would have to clean out the garage, so he just got to it. There was so much junk and trash to throw away. He began by sorting it into two piles: the throwaways and the stuff to be stored somewhere else. When he finally got through it all, the throwaway pile was twice the size of the stuff to be stored.

He gave the car a quick going-over and he knew the battery was dead, and maybe it was totally gone. He put the battery charger on it, and sure enough, it wasn't going to take a charge. He took it out and placed it in the truck. He realized the tires were flat and set about starting the air compressor. When the compressor was charged up enough, he went around and filled the tires up. As luck would have it, all the tires seemed to be holding air. He then rolled it out of the garage and parked it in the driveway. The car was covered with a thick, sticky dust with a mixture of chicken droppings. He grabbed the garden hose and a large scrub brush, and the cleaning started to show the true color of the car. Afterward, he rolled down the windows to freshen the stale stench that was a curse to the nose. Figuring that would take some time to work, he decided to head into town for a new battery. He called to Kipper, who was cooling in the shade of the old oak tree, loaded him up, and within seconds, they were whizzing down the road for town.

After purchasing the battery and making a quick stop at the local café for two hamburgers to-go, they were once again on the road for home. One hamburger, without anything on it, was for Kipper. With only one bite, it was plain out of sight. Bill laughed and slowly devoured his. They arrived home within a very short time; Kipper was back in the shade, and the battery was installed. Bill knew that the gas was bad in the tank and had to remove the tank to drain it. As he pulled the tank out from beneath the car, the sound of an approaching car came up the driveway. It was Sam and Mrs. Thomas from the day of shopping. Looking at his watch, it was almost five. *Where has the day gone?* Bill thought to himself. As the two ladies departed her vehicle, roars of laughter screamed from them. Hearing the commotion once again, Bill thought to himself, *Must have been a good time.* Kipper was now at Bill's side, ready to welcome back the long-lost shoppers.

"Oh, Granddad, what a great time I had. Thanks so much for letting me enjoy this day. Wait till I show you all the things I got," Sam said, beaming from pure joy. "What are you doing with the car?"

"I can't wait! Just thought I needed to get it running again," Bill responded.

Mrs. Thomas piped in, "Sam, go on in and put your stuff away. I need to talk with your grandfather for a while."

With that said, Sam grabbed all of her bags and headed into the house. She watched Sam as she went into the house and then turned to Bill.

"Thanks for such an enjoyable day. We must do this again soon," Mrs. Thomas said as she turned to Bill and smiled. "What an awesome granddaughter you have. We had so much fun. I see now that she hasn't had anyone before taking the time to spend with her. She is very special, and I will appeal to the courts for her to get her driver's license. Thanks again for such a wonderful day. I probably won't be coming out much more unless a serious problem arises or Sam wants to go shopping again. Goodbye!"

"Thanks for all you do, and feel free to stop by anytime," Bill said with a wide smile. He and Kipper stood by the driveway as they watched her pull away.

Bill looked down at Kipper and spoke, "We better go and see what all Sam brought home." With a quick wag of the tail, Kipper was heading for the door. Bill slowly walked up to the back door and stopped for a moment. He turned around and thought he caught a hint of Sara's favorite perfume. Once again, Bill realized that Sara was still watching over them. He turned, walked into the house, and headed for Sam's room. Within the next hour, Sam showed Bill everything she had gotten. Bill realized that the pieces of the puzzle were fitting into place.

The weekend flew by, and Bill found himself at the high school, registering Sam for her junior year of high school. Once he announced who he was there for, the administrator told him to take a seat over by the wall and that there was a person he was going to have to meet with.

A middle-aged man came walking up to Bill and said, "Good morning, I'm Steven Moore. I will be Samantha's counselor. I have been briefed on Samantha's situation by the courts. She is to report to me when she first arrives at school, and I have to ensure that she gets back on the bus. I have been informed that she is not to drive or be driven to school, except with you, unless the court changes its directives. I have received Samantha's makeup classes that she completed this summer, and I feel that she will fit in with our curriculum. You only have a few papers to sign, and we will send home with you the listing of selective classes that she can choose from. It's best to get these back to us as soon as possible; some of these classes fill up pretty fast. One last thing—we are to report to the court any disruption that she may cause. Do you have any questions for me?"

"Well, Mr. Moore, I respect the position that has been placed on you, but first let me say that when Sam was placed in my custody, she was given a clean slate. She has shown nothing but the greatest improvement in attitude and willingness to learn. I will not allow her past, as a bad seed, to cause negative attitudes toward her. I would hope that you will understand that I should be the first person to contact if any problems arise. She had lived a life of not being wanted or cared for. She should be treated with the same respect as any other student. I also expect that anyone with the attitude or reputation of a bad person will not be allowed to follow her. She just wants people to care about her. I would be very appreciative that we stayed in contact concerning her time here at school. I also hope that she will be allowed to participate in any sports that she decides to do," Bill spoke with a strong voice.

Mr. Moore, taken back by the firm conversation, said, "I assure you that we will provide the best education possible. I will convey your feelings to all of Sam's teachers and faculty members. The lady over at the desk has the needed paperwork for you to sign and take home. Thanks for coming. Hope to talk with you again. Goodbye."

Bill turned and walked over to the lady at the desk, signed the necessary paperwork, and took with him the list of selective classes for Sam to choose from. When he arrived home, he found Sam and Kipper out in the orchard, picking apples. He called over to her and had her come inside to go over what went on at school. After finishing up the conversation with Mr. Moore, Sam grabbed the course sheet and a pencil, sat down at the table, and started marking classes that she wanted to take. Being left out of the conversation, Kipper was doing his best to gain Sam's attention. He finally realized that she was busy and decided to go lay on his favorite blanket.

Sam had three weeks before the start of her junior year of high school. Realizing that she had to socialize with new fellow students was exciting. Just as Sam and Kipper were lounging around the front room, the phone rang. Since Sam wasn't allowed to use the phone, Bill had to answer it. She could hear him speak.

"Hello? Oh. Hi…Oh, that's awesome news. …I can't wait to tell her. Thanks so much. Yes, I will. Goodbye!"

She then heard the click of the phone. Bill walked into the room with a wide grin on his face.

"What is it?" she anxiously questioned him.

"We need to start teaching you how to drive the truck. The courts approved your request for a driver's license. Mrs. Thomas has scheduled you to take the Edison Driving School that starts next Monday. We need to run by them and pick up the driver's course study guide. You know, you have to pass the written exam before you take the driving course."

Before Bill could speak again, Sam jumped off the couch and into Bill's arms. He could feel the wetness from the tears streaming down her face.

"Okay, let's get ready. We can take Kipper and go get that study guide."

With one last squeeze, she released him and said to Kipper, "Last one to the truck is a rotten egg!"

Kipper, sensing the excitement, started to jump around, barking. As Bill and Sam started for the backdoor, Kipper had already beat them to it. All three loaded up in the truck, and they headed for the Edison Driving School. After they arrived, they found out that she would be taking evening classes from 6:00 p.m. to 8:00 p.m., Monday through Friday, for two weeks. Then, after successfully passing the written exam, she would start five Saturday driving tests, two hours each. Bill thought about celebrating the occasion, so on the way home, they stopped at the local pizza joint for much-deserved pizza. Kipper was already allowed in as a customer, so he laid by the table and ate the various pieces of crust that they threw at him. With the pizza devoured, the three loaded back up and took the final phase of the journey home.

The following week, Sam studied the driving guide from cover to cover, taking several notes along the way. When Monday came for the start of the course, she was ready and willing to take on the task.

While Sam was in class, Bill went to the local town library and read the various newspapers and magazines. The final class was done, and Sam had taken the written test, which she passed with flying colors. Next Saturday, she would start the five-day driving test. Before they started, Bill had taught Sam how to drive both the car with an automatic transmission and the old truck with a standard transmission. With gears grinding and several stalls of the engine, she finally got the feel for driving the truck.

With the excitement of the driving course, Sam didn't realize that school started the following Monday. Without a doubt, it came in the blink of an eye. She was up early that Monday morning, dressed and ready for the bus. Bill tried to calm her down a little bit, for it would be another hour and a half before the bus would arrive. Then the time came for her to walk the long driveway to the road. With Kipper walking by her side, he was keeping Sam company till she entered her new world.

The big yellow bus came to an abrupt stop, and the door swung open. The lady driver was named Maxine and had driven this route for the past twenty-seven years. Not one for small chit-chat, she gave Sam a smile and motioned for her to take a seat. With Sam sitting down, Maxine closed the door, and the bus lunged forward as it took off like a rocket. After many stops along the way, it finally pulled up in front of the high school, and all the students got off. When Sam exited the bus, Mr. Moore was standing there waiting for her.

"Samantha Roberts, hi, I'm Mr. Moore. I'm assigned to be your school counselor. I'm the one who talked with your grandfather. You have the same class schedule as Sherry Martin. She will be joining you in the commons area and showing you the way to your classes. If you have any questions, feel free to ask. Do you have any questions now?

Sam just shook her head. "Come with me, and I'll take you to Sherry." With that said, he led her inside the building and into the commons area. He walked up to Sherry, who was standing with several other students.

"Ms. Martin, this is Samantha Roberts, the young lady I was talking about. I will leave her in your hands. Take good care of her." When Mr. Moore finished, he turned around and walked away.

"Hi Samantha," Sherry said as she smiled and held out her hand. Sam took a hold of it and gave it a quick shake. "So where are you coming from?"

"Silver Lake," Sam said in a low-tone voice.

"I've been there several times. I hope you're going to like it here at Wabaunsee High School. It has its problems, but mostly good times." The bell rang. "That's the first bell. We need to head to our first class." Sherry led the way, with Sam following behind her.

Through the various classes that she attended the first day, Sam's head was a blur with all the students and teachers that she met. With the last class completed, Sherry, still by her side, walked her out to her bus.

Sherry turned and said to Sam, "I hope you enjoyed the day. If you ever need anything or have questions, don't hesitate to give me a shout. I got to go back in, I'm doing some posters for our upcoming football game. Maybe you can help sometime. Okay, bye!" Sam gave a quick wave of the hand, and Sherry was gone.

Riding alone in a seat on the bus, Sam had heavy thoughts of that day in school. She felt that this might work out. The students and teachers gave the impression of caring for each other and being willing to help. What a difference she felt compared to the last school year. The bus came to a jarring stop, and Sam came back to reality to find herself at her get-off spot.

Kipper was there to greet her, which gave Sam a tear in her eye. She knew without a doubt that someone really missed and cared for her. Jumping around like a darn fool, Kipper couldn't control his excitement about having Sam back home. They walked back up the long driveway and found Bill on the porch to welcome her back.

"Well, how did it go?" Bill said with a smile.

"Not too bad!" Sam replied back. "Mr. Moore met me when I got off the bus, and he introduced me to Sherry Martin. She has the same classes as I do. She escorted me to all the classes, and we shared lunch together. She was really nice. I forgot about having to do homework, and I've got a lot to do."

"It's all part of it," Bill said as he opened the door for Sam and Kipper. "If you need any help with any of it, maybe I can help. You know, it's been a long time since I was in school," he said as he walked in.

"Thanks, Grandpa. Thanks for caring!" Sam said this with tears working up in her eyes. She then set her bookbag down on the table. She opened the refrigerator door and scanned the contents of it for a quick snack. "Tell me, Grandpa. What was school like for you? Did you enjoy it or was it something you had to do?" she said as she pulled a bowl of grapes from the refrigerator.

Bill pondered the thought for a moment and then softly spoke, "School was nothing that I really wanted to do. My sister, Laura, had to help me with a lot of the English stuff. I was good in math and didn't care a whole lot about government classes, but I got by. Then I met her! A goddess from my dreams, your grandmother. My heart always skipped a beat when I saw her. School was important to her, and so it became important to me. Every waking moment, she was all I thought of. I lost many nights' sleeps just thinking about her."

Bill had gotten Sam's full attention.

"I don't remember much about her. I remember her coming over to the house, but I was so young and really didn't realize who she was. She was so sweet, but I don't remember you ever being with her," Sam said as she searched Bill's eyes for answers.

Bill took a long sigh as he looked out the window, waiting for Sara to give him an answer to her question.

"I guess I was too busy to make time for you and your family. Grandma always made sure that she was there for everyone. I'm sure she made excuses for me, but I wasn't there for anyone. As they say, hindsight is so much greater than foresight." He could feel tears swelling up in his eyes. Kipper, sensing his emotion, went by his side and licked his hand. Bill, in return, gave Kipper a few rubs on his head.

Sam then said, "Do you have any photo albums or boxes of pictures that I can look at?"

Bill nodded his head yes and said, "They are in the hall closet on the top shelf. Haven't had them out for such a long time. Long before Sara had left...me." He couldn't speak anymore. The feelings had gotten to him, and he turned and walked out the back door with Kipper by his side.

Sam knew that he had to have time for himself. She now really knew how much she meant to him. She also knew that she wanted to know more about her and what she was to her mom and Uncle Justin. Maybe, just maybe, she could be the right reason to bring the family back together. She had eaten enough grapes, so she placed the bowl back in the refrigerator and headed to the hall closet. This was the first time she had opened the door and came face-to-face with a pure mess. It was surprising that nothing had fallen out with so much stuff packed in it. As she moved most of the stuff in the front out onto the hall floor, she spied a blue shoebox on the top shelf. When she pulled it out and opened the lid, it was full of military items. She pulled out a small case and opened it. It was a medal with a ribbon of light blue. At the center of the piece was an American eagle above a star. Above the eagle was a light-blue octagonal patch with thirteen stars on it. Also inside the case was a folded-up paper. It started out with "The United States of America," then, following other comments in large bold letters, "Medal of Honor." His name was written on the certificate. Sam knew of the importance of this award but didn't know that he even served in the military. All she could do was marvel at the medal. She finally pulled herself away from it and continued to comb through the shoebox. She came across a dozen or so medals scattered about in the box. She couldn't wait to approach him about these items.

It was over an hour before Bill and Kipper returned to the house. Bill found her sitting at the table with the blue shoebox.

"Grandpa, tell me about the items in this box," Sam said with anticipation of surreal stories.

"What's in the box?" Bill asked as he opened the lid. "Oh, I haven't seen these items in many, many years. Probably before Justin was even born. Not much to tell, and almost all of them, along with fifty cents, gets you a cup of coffee at the café."

"Grandpa, this one is the Medal of Honor!" Sam blurted out.

"Yeah, it was a big thing going to the White House and having President Johnson pin it on me. What about the people who came home in a pine box? The president didn't greet their bodies when they came home. I lost a lot of good friends over there, and what I got didn't make up for the friendships that I lost. Your grandma knew how I felt and just placed them away, and we both forgot about them. I haven't forgotten my buddies who didn't come home alive. That's about all

I have to say about the items in the box. They are yours if you want them," Bill said as he looked at Sam with a solemn face.

"Okay, Grandpa, enough said," Sam spoke as she closed the lid to the box, took it, and put it in her room.

The next couple of months flew by, with Sam passing her driver's test and now in possession of a driver's license. School was working out well for her, especially since she met Derrick. Derrick was tall, dark, and handsome. He was a star football player, and he cherished the ground Sam walked on. Sam was hesitant to bring up Derrick with Bill. One night at dinner, Sam let it slip out Derrick was making her laugh in social studies class. That's when Bill picked up on the boyfriend thing.

"So, who is this Derrick guy?" Bill said as he took a bite of spaghetti.

"Oh, he's just a boy that I got to know in school," Sam said in a sheepish voice. "Did I tell you that they want me to play basketball?"

"No, you didn't, but don't change the subject. Is Derrick cute?" Bill asked with a slight grin. "What do you know about him?" Bill knew that boy discussions would sooner or later be the topic at mealtime.

"Yes, he's very cute and one of the best football players on the team. Do you think we could go to a football game? They are playing here this Friday night."

"I think that could be possible. I believe you need to get out more. You know, I'll have to check with Mrs. Thomas and get her take on it, but I don't see any problem with it," Bill said as he took another bite of food. "I'll call her tomorrow morning. If you got homework, I'll do the dishes."

"Yeah, I do," she said as she took a drink of milk.

The rest of the night was consumed by Sam's homework, Bill doing dishes and laundry, and Kipper laying on his favorite blanket. The next morning after Sam had left for school, Bill gave Mrs. Thomas a call and got the approval for Sam's new love interest and going to the Friday night football game. With a blink of an eye, Friday night came, and Sam was so excited. Bill thought back on how many of Justin's games he had missed and wished he could live that part of his life all over. Bill was sitting by himself, for Sam had gone and was sitting with Sherry and all her friends. They won their game, and Sam went down from the bleachers and met up with Derrick. She signaled for Bill to come down and meet him. He was a tall, good-looking young man, who was very polite and courteous. Bill told Sam he would meet her at the truck when she was ready to leave. Bill could tell when he saw Sam coming that her feet weren't touching the ground. She was walking on cloud nine.

Days were now turning into weeks, and the months were nothing but blurs. Bill was talking with Julie more and more, keeping her informed of all Sam was doing. Christmas was especially good, for Derrick and Sam spent time together both at Bill's house and Derrick's parents' house. Julie loaded Bill up with lots of presents for both him and Sam. There were even a few for Kipper. Bill was keeping busy keeping the driveway and sidewalks clear of snow, where Kipper was finding pure joy bouncing through it. One day, after shoveling off the walkway, he came in and sat down at the kitchen table. Sam came in and sat across the table from him.

"Grandpa, I want to talk to Mom," she said in a soft voice. "Do you think you could work your magic and get the court's permission for me to talk to her? I think I have proven myself worthy of it. I want to tell her about Derrick, school, and how much I miss her!"

"You have more than proven yourself. I'm so happy that you are at this point to reconnect with your mom. You know, I have kept her informed of all that you do, and I know it would make her heart swell to know that you want to talk with her. I will do everything that I can to make that happen," Bill said with a twinkle in his eyes.

Sam's face was now flowing with tears of joy. Since it was Saturday, he knew that he shouldn't call Mrs. Thomas on her day off, but what the heck, it was worth a try. He went into the front room and picked up the phone. Within seconds, Mrs. Thomas answered the phone and was glad that he called. After explaining that Sam wanted to talk to her mom, she was pleased to inform him that she had already gotten permission for Sam to call her mom. She wanted to hear that Sam wanted to talk with her before she said anything about it. Bill said he understood and was grateful for getting permission. With the end of the conversation, he hung up the phone and pondered if Sara was the one making things happen. He picked up the phone again and dialed Julie's number. Within a couple of rings, Julie answered. He told her to hold on for a moment and then handed the phone to Sam. As Sam was about to speak, Bill leaned down and kissed Sam on the forehead. Then he and Kipper went outside.

"Mom, this is Sam," she said in a trembling voice.

CHAPTER 8

A BIRTHDAY FOR SARA

"Sam!" And then there was the sound of sobbing. "Are you supposed to be talking with me?" Julie's voice was breaking up.

"Yes, Grandpa got permission for me to be able to talk with you," Sam replied.

"How are you? I missed you so much." Julie's voice then went silent.

"I miss you too! I have so much to tell you. My life is filled with so many things now. I almost don't know what all to tell. I've made some really good friends in school. One of them is named Derrick; he's cute. I got my driver's license. Mom, I've learned so much and realize that I matter in the world."

"That is so great to hear. I've been praying for you, and it seems that they are all coming true. I also have been rearranging my life too. I'm getting my priorities in order and dumping all my stupidities out the door. Wait, what? Who is this Derrick? You say he's cute?" Julie said surprisingly.

"Oh my, yes! He is one of the best football players on the team. He comes over here once in a while, and I have dinner with him and his parents on occasion. Grandpa really likes him too." Sam continued to fill Julie in on all that had gone on.

The phone conversation went on for over an hour. At the end of the conversation, both Sam and Julie's emotions got the best of them. For a few short minutes, all they could do was cry. Finally done with the farewells, they hung up the phone. Sam ran into her bedroom and cried into the night. Bill could hear her crying and knew it was best to leave her alone. She needed to heal her pain and release her emotions.

The end of the school year was upon them, and Sam's year of probation was ending. Mrs. Thomas called Bill into her office to evaluate the final exposition that would be presented to the judge. Mrs. Thomas had gotten a preliminary set of school transcripts for Sam's classes. She was in the upper part of her class, with rave reviews from her teachers. The main concern for Bill and Mrs. Thomas was whether Sam would stay with him or move back into her mother's house. They both felt that Sam had grown beyond her past but wondered if changing schools and friends would be best for her. It was up to the judge to decide that, and within a week they would know Sam's fate.

The court date was set for Tuesday of the following week at 2:00 p.m. The court summoned everyone concerned. Bill and Sam were the first to arrive, followed by Julie and then Clint. Mrs. Thomas was soon to follow. Surprising everyone, Derrick and his parents walked in. Within a very short time, the court was in session.

The judge first spoke, "I have read the exposition on behalf of Samantha Roberts, and I have to say, I am totally impressed with the outcome of this past year. Ms. Roberts, you have proven beyond a doubt that you can be trusted and are a very smart young lady. I decree that the restriction placed on you be lifted. Now the concern of the court is, where do you want to live? Ms. Roberts, I ask you now."

Sam stood up and looked at her mom and then at Bill. She slowly spoke, "I wish to stay with my grandfather but would like to be able to stay with my mom on occasion. I love the school that I'm at and desperately want to complete my senior year there. I also would like to say that this past year has proven to me that people do care about me. If it weren't for everyone concerned, I would be locked away and forgotten. I am grateful to the court for giving me the opportunity to change my way of life and to prove myself worthy."

The judge nodded her head in agreement and then spoke, "The people in your life who have looked after you are the ones to be grateful for. Mrs. Thomas has kept me informed of all your achievements throughout the year. I am proud of you, and all I can say is that I find you worthy of being who you are, and this case is now closed. You are free to live wherever you want. Case dismissed!"

The courtroom erupted in cheers and shouts. Sam jumped up and hugged Bill. Julie came running over and joined in the hug. Within seconds, the whole group was surrounding Sam. All were congratulating Sam; not many dry eyes were to be found.

Clint was the exception in the group. He seemed to sense that he didn't matter and confronted Bill over the matter. He quickly asked Bill why he took in Sam when he was never there before for her. Sam noticed the conversation between the two and jumped in.

"I know I made a big mistake, but life with you and Mother hasn't been much of a life. Grandfather has shown me more attention and respect than I have gotten in years."

"You know that's not true. Hell, when was the last time your grandfather came by and sent you a present for your birthday or Christmas?"

Sam blurted back, "How many times did you take me to see my grandfather, or even let me talk to him on the phone? If you're not going to be part of the solution, then at least don't be part of the problem. I'm going to do what Grandfather wants, and if you don't like it, then get out."

Clint was taken by surprise by how Sam was talking to him. She had never raised her voice to him.

He turned and faced Julie and said, "What's your feeling on this?"

Julie looked at him with tears welling in her eyes. "My father is a great father, and I know he's an even greater grandfather. It's my fault that I never included him in our lives. He agreed to let Sam live with him and taught her life. It was our only choice to keep Sam out of prison. We made a mess of our relationship and the home life of our child."

Clint, with tears in his eyes, nodded his head in agreement and said, "You're right."

He slowly turned and faced Bill, held out his hand, and softly spoke, "I'm sorry, I'm talking nonsense. So sorry Bill, for not allowing you to share our family. Sam is able to hold her head high because of what you did. I'm sorry for not realizing that. Please forgive me." He then held out his hand in friendship.

Bill took a hold of Clint's hand and gave him a firm handshake. "Don't ever think that she needs me more than you. She needs every one of us. Only through love, understanding, and yes, prayers, will we ensure that she gets the life that she deserves."

Bill and Clint nodded their heads in agreement while Sam grabbed both her father and grandfather's arms. She held on to them tight, as if to never, ever let them go.

With that said, Julie headed out the door to retrieve her phone from the turn-in station. Bill was sensing an ease of tension and took a moment to think of Sara and if what had transpired would have met her approval. He felt the presence of her love descend upon him. He knew without a doubt that he had done well. He glanced back over to Sam and saw her looking back at him with a smile. When he gazed upon Clint, the look on his face was one of disbelief at what had just happened. Caught up in all the commotion, Clint wasn't sure of anything right now. Bill was glad that he was allowed back into a family that had so long ago left him behind.

Sensing the time, Clint looked back at Bill and asked, "Bill, would you like to go get something to eat? I haven't had anything this morning, and I got a feeling it's going to be a long day. Plus, I'd like to do some catching up with you on things."

Bill nodded his head and said, "Not real hungry, but a cup of coffee and conversation would do me good."

Clint turned to Sam and said, "Honey, would you like to come join us? We will only be gone for a short time."

By this time, Derrick and his parents were with Sam.

Sam spoke, "Sorry, Dad. I am going with Derrick and his parents for a celebration dinner. Maybe soon we will get together and catch up on things." Sam smiled and gave her father a hug. "Thanks, Daddy."

She then turned to Bill. "Thanks, Grandpa. Thanks for your faith in me." As she grabbed a hold of him, she gave him a hug also.

Clint asked, "Do you have any particular place in mind where you want to get some coffee?"

Bill smiled and said, "My stomach is telling me no more coffee today, it needs food. Anywhere is fine with me."

"I know a small Mexican fast-food place down here on west Sixth Street called Taco House. They serve the best enchiladas and taco burgers around. I've been going there since I was in grade school. I've known the owner for many, many years. His grandson and Sam were close friends in school."

"Sounds good to me," Bill said with a grin.

It wasn't too long before Bill and Clint arrived at the place and were quickly served. As they were finishing up their meals, Clint's phone rang again.

"Clint, this is the office, and you have a client appointment at 1:00 p.m.," came the voice at the other end. "The boss doesn't want you to miss this one; he's one of our biggest customers." Clint recognized the voice as Sheree, the office manager, and then remembered the appointment.

"Sheree, I won't be able to make it. Do me a favor and call Mr. Dent and relay to him that I will reschedule the appointment in the next couple of days."

"Mr. Johnson said you would probably try to weasel out of this appointment. He said that if you don't make this appointment, don't bother coming in." With that, the phone went dead. Clint knew that with his past experiences, he had burned his bridges with his company and was on the verge of being without a job. Clint now was facing another challenge of life's revenge. Not knowing for sure what to do, he now confided in Bill.

"You're in the center of the hurricane," Bill came back with. "You've come back to the reality of being a father who cares, working a job that pays the bills, and keeping your livelihood alive. Sam should be the most important aspect of your life, but the job is the means to be able to support her through this time of need, not including making ends meet at home. Take that appointment; I'll take care of the check."

"Thanks, Bill," Clint said as he dialed the office and told them he would meet with Mr. Dent. Upon Clint finishing up the conversation, he got up and headed out the door. It wasn't long before Bill paid the check and headed out the door to return home. As he drove home, he felt a feeling of relief that Sam's situation had come to a close. He began to wonder what would come next. At least he knew that he had Sam for another year. With the chains removed from her, how would she respond to her new freedom? Only time would tell. With his mind full of these thoughts, he arrived home with Kipper wagging his tail with excitement.

As he walked up to the house, Bill spoke to Kipper, "Well, old boy, she is free, and a lot of credit goes to you. I couldn't have done it without you. Sam has set a new life for herself, Julie has realized her mistakes, and Clint has grown back into being a father. Kinda wonder how we are going to handle this situation."

Kipper's response was to just jump around like a nut as he usually did.

Derrick brought Sam home around seven-thirty and by the look in Sam's eyes, it just had to be love. As she walked around the house humming a tune, Bill knew for sure it was love. Later on that evening, Sam took Sara's photo down off the mantel and stared at it for a very long time. Turning to Bill with tears in her eyes, she said, "You loved her with all your heart, how have you handled the pain?"

Bill, sitting in his chair with Kipper's head in his lap, responded, "I haven't! Only memories of her have kept me from dying from the pain," Bill said without looking up. "From the very first day I met her, I felt totally blessed." Bill looked at Sam and spoke again, "Then that fateful day came, and I heard her voice no more; the golden touch of her hand was not to be felt again. I cursed the world that day. I could no longer handle anything. I went numb from life; I could not feel the existence of any emotions. I just wanted to di..." Bill's eyes were swollen, and tears were flowing down his face.

Kipper sensed his tormented feelings, raised his head, and placed it next to Bill's. Bill wrapped his arms around him, sobbing uncontrollably. Sam walked over to him and knelt down next to Kipper. With one arm around Kipper and the other around Bill, she cried the tears of unknown love.

Sam broke the embrace and silence by standing up and wiping the tears from her face. She stood there for a moment and then her face brightened up a little and said, "Let's get everyone together and give grandma a birthday party!"

"A birthday party?" Bill said with a gasp. "Honey, she's been gone almost eight years!"

"Grandpa, I know that, but what a way to honor her memory! Her birthday is a month and a half away, and by that time, I'm sure we could get everyone together for it. We could have it at her gravesite and share our memories of Grandma. Wouldn't it be great to have everyone together? I was very young when Grandma passed, so I only remember a few things about her. If everyone shared their memories, then I could know more about her. What are your thoughts on this?"

"Are you talking about Justin, too?" Bill spoke with hesitation.

"Of course," Sam said with a gleam in her eyes.

As soon as Sam said this, Kipper jumped up from his position on the floor and began to jump around, barking loudly. Neither one had a clue what brought this on, but both were laughing at Kipper's actions. Bill was quick to realize that Sam was up to something, but what it was, he wasn't quite sure. It would seem by the way Kipper was acting that he was in on the plan too. Bill gave a quick sigh and laid his head back on the chair. Within seconds, he decided to just let Sam figure this one out.

Sam's head was a whirlwind with all the ideas she had for the party. She was thrilled to death with thoughts of the family being together once again. Sam quickly went to the back door in the kitchen, and Kipper was in hot pursuit. Who knew what these two would conjure up? But Bill knew it would be something special. As soon as they reached the back-yard, Kipper grabbed his favorite tug-of-war rag and challenged Sam to take it. He was dancing around like a darn fool, keeping Sam just out of reach. Finally, Sam just laid down on the ground with her eyes closed. Kipper cautiously approached Sam with the rag still in his mouth. Just as Kipper reached her, she jumped up, grabbed Kipper, and laid him down on the ground. Kipper wasn't surprised by this action, for he knew it was all part of the game that they played.

The very next day, Sam was up bright and early, working on writing out everything that would be needed for Sara's birthday party—where and how everything would happen and people who needed to be contacted. Her thoughts were only interrupted by Bill calling her in for breakfast.

As she entered the kitchen, Bill smiled and asked, "How's the birthday planning going?"

"I think I've got it all figured out," she said with a grin. "I need to run into town, so can I borrow the truck?"

"I'll take you," Bill said.

"Sorry, I have a couple of things that I don't want you to know about," she said as she fixed her toast.

"Oh, I get it; something with Derrick," Bill quickly replied back.

"Yep, you got it figured right," Sam said as she winked her eye.

"Here are the car keys; be gentle with her. I've had her a long time." Sam didn't realize he had the car up and running. "The keys are yours; don't lose them," Bill said as he returned the wink.

She went over to him, grabbed the keys, and gave him a kiss. "Thank you, Grandpa, for everything."

Bill watched as Sam took off for her bedroom and wondered what she was up to. As he got up, Kipper was waiting at the door for their morning walk. They mostly strolled around the yard, checking out the various flowers or vegetables in the garden. As they were walking through the garden, he noticed Sam heading for the car. Within minutes, she was heading down the driveway. Several hours had passed before Bill saw the car coming. Sam came into the kitchen and then headed for her bedroom.

"What's going on?" Bill asked.

Sam turned around and said, "Nothing special, just taking care of business."

"Did you meet with Derrick?" he asked.

"Nope, he was helping his dad with the chores. Talk to you later; got a birthday party to plan," Sam said as she returned to the direction of her bedroom.

Bill went to the kitchen and glanced at the calendar. Sara's birthday was June twenty-nine, so he thought to himself, *Less than a month away. Not much time to plan a party. Oh well, it's her party, and I'm sure it will be a great one.* He went back into the front room and sat in his favorite chair. He gazed out the window and went into deep thoughts about his beloved Sara. Her image reappeared in his mind, and she was walking through a field, picking wildflowers. It was as though she were inviting him to take the walk with her. She seemed to be happy that he appeared to be with her. Oh, how he wished he could hold her in his arms once again. His return to reality came when Sam came into the room. She had gathered several of the photo albums that were stored away in the hall closet. She sat down on the couch and motioned for him to join her.

"Grandpa, please go through these with me. I would really like to know more about the people and places that are in these photos," Sam asked.

"Well, it's been a long time since I looked at these. I'll try my best to remember who they all are. Let's start with the earliest album and work our way up to the most recent. That one over there with the flowers on it, I believe, is the oldest one."

She handed him that one, and he opened it up and sighed.

He pointed to one of the pictures and said, "Those two were my parents. The next one here is with me and all my brothers and sister. This one is Charles, the oldest. We think he moved to California. Next is Leroy, or as we call him, Roy. He lives in Alta Vista. Don't talk to him very often. That's Laura; she married a Marine and is living in Hawaii with their two children. Her husband died a few years back. That's me and my youngest brother, Thomas. He moved to California to live with my brother Charles."

"In the cemetery, there is a grave marker with Cheri Lynn Schyular; was she a sister?" Sam asked.

"Yes, she was the youngest. She died in childbirth. My mother never got over losing her," Bill said as he continued combing through the album pages. After going through most of the albums, Sam stopped Bill when they came across a picture of Mrs. Davis.

"Who was she? She wasn't family, was she?" Sam asked seriously.

"She wasn't blood family, but she was definitely family. She was always there for all of us when we needed someone. She helped Mother when Cheri died. She came and helped me when I was still in school and living all alone. She took care of me like a mother would," Bill said as he wiped a tear from his eye just thinking of her.

"Why is she buried in the family cemetery?" Sam asked.

"It was the desire of her family and mine, for she was very special to all of us," Bill replied.

Sam knew that enough was said and moved on. They finished going through all of the albums, with Sam pulling several pictures out and laying them in a pile on the coffee table.

"What are you going to do with them?"

"I want to study them some more; I really want to know the family I came from," Sam said as she picked up the photos and walked to her room.

The very next day, Sam put into motion the invitations for the party. She started by calling her mom.

"Mom, this is Sam." After a short time of small talk, Sam revealed her reason for calling. "I'm planning a birthday party for Grandma. I know so very little about her, and I want to get everyone together at her gravesite. We could all share our memories of her. I need for you to contact Justin and have his family there. I know Grandpa and Justin haven't talked in so many years. I thought maybe they could clear the air between them."

"Honey, I don't think that's a very good idea. But I'll give it a try; can't guarantee he will come," Julie said with skepticism in her voice.

Sam finished making the other invitations by sending letters out to Leroy and Laura, even though neither one really kept in contact with Bill. With all the makings of the party and time spent with Derrick, Sam was so busy that she hadn't spent much time with Kipper. He was wondering why their play time had gone away.

The days and weeks were flying by, and finally the day arrived. Julie and Clint arrived early to help set things up. They brought some lawn chairs and a folding table, if needed. She also brought a large bowl of potato salad. Bill got the barbecue grill ready and had hamburgers and hot dogs for the main course. Kipper was running around them all, for he knew this was going to be a very special day. Once everything was in place, Julie and Clint sat down with Bill and Sam.

Julie spoke first, "We want you both to know that we have ended our differences and are taking counseling sessions to ensure our relationship will last. We have realized that we have placed both of you in a very bad situation. But it has made us see our failures in our past."

Clint then spoke, "How wrong I was, searching for something less than what I had at home. I love your mom more than I did when I married her. Sam, both you and your mom have brought more meaning to my life than I ever thought possible. Bill, I can't say how sorry I am for ignoring you all these years. You made this change in all our lives possible. Thank you!"

With not a dry eye between them all, they all took a moment to reflect on all that was said. They didn't even notice the SUV pulling up in the driveway. Cheryl Thomas and her husband, Tom, got out and walked up to Sam.

With a quick hug, Cheryl said, "Thanks so much for inviting us. This is one party I wouldn't want to miss. This is my husband, Tom."

Handshakes were quickly exchanged between them all. Then Sam and Bill motioned for all to gather around Sara's gravesite. Just as Sam was about to start the opening statement, another car pulled up in the driveway. When it stopped, a large frame of a man stepped out. Bill gasped when he turned around. It was Justin, followed by his wife and two sons.

Julie cried out, "Justin, you made it!"

Bill slowly walked out to him. Bill searched for words that should have been spoken long before now. When he got to Justin, he held out his hand and said, "I'm sorry for being such a fool."

Justin took his hand, pulled him over to him, and hugged him.

He whispered in his ear, "It was I who was a fool." Then he pulled away and looked him in the eyes, and then said, "Julie told me all that you have done for Sam. She made me realize that you were always doing what was right—that we never had a need for anything. I never saw it that way till I had a family of my own. I was too ashamed to face you and tell you that I was wrong."

Just as tears were about to flow, Sam and Julie came up to the two of them and went in for a group hug.

"Sam, this is your Uncle Justin. He's sometimes a pain in the butt, but we all love him just the same," Julie explained.

With the hugs all over, Justin motioned for his wife, Janet, and two sons, Dusty and Jason, over to meet his dad. With the introductions done, Bill realized that the others were waiting for them over by the grave. When the whole party had gathered together, Sam grabbed a bag and pulled out a handful of booklets that she had made up. She passed them out, and when people opened them, they were amazed at the pictures she had composed in them.

Sam took center stage and began celebrating Sara's birthday. "I am so honored to see you all here today. Today was Sara Schyuler's birthday. I don't really have many memories of her, but from what I can tell, she was the one and only for Grandpa. She was the mother of my mother and my Uncle Justin. She was the glue of the family. When she left this world, the family fell apart. Now, in her name, the glue has bonded once again, never to fall apart again. I asked you all to come today to share memories of her so I can know more about her. Hopefully, others that didn't know her will get knowledge of the love that she gave her family."

Throughout the next hour, the people who knew her shared very special memories of her. There were times of laughter and times of sorrow, but in the end, all were grateful for the words about Sara. All knew that Sara would live in their hearts forever. After all had been said about Sara, Sam stood up, grabbed the wrapped box, and handed it to Bill.

"What's this? It's not my birthday."

Sam responded, "Grandma told me to do this for you."

"Well, okay," Bill said. He opened up the box and pulled out a large shadow box. On top was the folded American flag and below was a box filled with all Bill's ribbons and medals. In the center, the beautiful Medal of Honor was hanging.

Bill looked up at her with a tear in his eye and said, "Why?"

"You served our country with honor and dignity. You respected your fallen brothers in combat and never forgot them. You had placed them higher than the awards received from our country. Grandma was with you every step of the way and never let you down. It's time for everyone to know of yours and Grandma's sacrifice in a time of unrest. I love you, Grandpa, and know I always will." Sam's eyes were flowing with tears, as were those of everyone standing there.

Justin and Julie rushed over to their father, holding the shadow box, and gazed upon it. Justin, choking back the tears, quickly spoke, "Dad, I never knew. You received the Congressional Medal of Honor? Why didn't you tell us?"

"I guess I felt that part of my life should be put away, for I was no hero; I just wanted to be a good man and provide for my family."

Julie went next to Bill and wrapped her arms around him.

"Dad, you are a hero—not only for your service to our country, but to our family and especially to Mom. We never had a need, with a roof over our heads, food for the table, and clothes on our backs, and you never failed to show Mom anything but love. Look what you have done for Sam. I don't know anyone who could have done what you have. Only now do I realize how much of a hero you really are. I'm sorry I never told you; I love you." Then she gently kissed him.

Janet, Dusty, and Jason walked up close to Bill and looked at the shadow box in total amazement.

Janet looked at Bill with tears in her eyes and said, "It is a true honor to get to know a man such as you. I never pressed Justin to learn about you; now I know. Your grandsons here will be part of your life as much as you will be part of ours." With that, she went up to him and gave him a kiss and a hug.

Bill, taken back by all this, couldn't control his emotions.

Finally gathering himself, he called out, "Let's get ready for something to eat."

Everyone moved over to the picnic table and lawn chairs. Justin's two boys were playing with Kipper, who was playing keep-away with them. Bill was getting the grill ready; Sam was talking with her mother and Janet. Cheryl and her husband were engaged in conversation with Justin. Bill scanned the site and knew that without Sara, this would not have been possible. Just as they sat down to enjoy the feast before them, Bill turned and saw a nice new truck pulling up in the driveway. When it stopped, he saw that it had California license plates. Two men stepped out of the truck and walked slowly up to the gathering.

On the porch, Kipper lifted his head as he watched the two men getting out of the truck. It was as if Kipper knew who they were. He had a smile on his face as he laid his head back down on the worn-out blanket. All was well in the family that he loved.

ABOUT THE AUTHOR

Throughout my time on the oceans and seas, my eyes were witnesses to so many things. Some were good, and some were not so good. I wish not to change a single thing. What I've learned in my life has made me who I am. The thing that bothers me the most is that life is stolen from so many children who were not able to experience life to its fullest and were not holding onto that hand of love. Children need to be taught the ways of the world and to explore the challenges and wonders of so many things. I might be crusty and sometimes crude, but I still have a heart that bleeds for the tears of the lonely. Life is too short for abuse or neglect.

Captain McDoogle
BB